The Pass

Also by Lorne Oliver

Lorne Oliver

The Pass

An Alcrest Mystery

THE PASS

Copyright © 2016 by Lorne Oliver

ISBN: 978-0-9940309-0-0

Cover Painting: Ej Anarchy
Cover Design: C.D. Breadner

Brandi

I love you more today than yesterday,

Not as much as tomorrow.

Acknowledgments

I have to start things off with thanking Brandi, Jordann and Wylie for their love and support.

Thank you to EJ Anarchy for the amazing work of art which became the cover and CD Breadner for making it into a cover. Thank you Donna for your work. As you edit, I learn. Cheryl, you have been a great support.

Elizabeth Frances, as always, thank you for the inspiration.

To anyone who reads and reviews my work, you have no idea what that means to an author. We are in our own worlds and to find out we did a good job makes it all worthwhile.

To the voices in my head – keep talking to me.

Shortly before publishing this book my friend Beau Waitforit Regard passed away. He was the real Bullet the Bulldog. He was my friend.

Pass

To move on

To come to an end

The area in a restaurant where plates are handed off
from kitchen to server

Chapter 1

"This is fucking crazy," Spencer Alcrest slipped off the pew onto the kneeler. He quickly remembered the rhyme, "spectacles, testicles, wallet and watch," as he made the sign of the cross.

His sister, Chrys, glared at him but didn't move. Hopefully, with the noise of people kneeling no one heard. The lady half of the older couple sitting next to them had already tsk'd them a couple of times. A few women in the front wailed, while others in the room sniffled. The prayer finished, Amen's were said. Everyone sat back in the pews, the wood creaked, and the priest continued. Chrys nibbled her lip and rubbed her hands together between her thighs. They were all sweaty. She hated churches and despised funerals. She finally glanced beside her. The tsk-er lady was shaking her head waiting for one of them to look so she could stop.

Spencer had returned to his pissed-off stance with arms crossed over his chest, back solid against the back of the pew, lips pursed together and eyes staring at the man in robes speaking at the pulpit.

There was no casket today. To the left of the stage were large framed photographs of the woman who had the church full of mourners. She had a round face and long dark hair that either cascaded over her shoulders in black waves or was in a tight braid depending on the photo. In one her hair must have been in a bun at the top of her head because she wore a white stove-top paper chef hat. No matter what photo, the woman had a brilliant smile that seemed to radiate through full cheeks and dark eyes. If the photo's moved like in the world of Harry Potter books, Chrys imagined the thirty year old woman would have been laughing, maybe even singing. Inside the entrance to the church was another display of personal photographs. In each of those she, again, was smiling and laughing. One had Spencer and two other friends in it – all four showing off their new tattoos for the camera. Spencer's tattoo was a lobster crawling around his right elbow, Tessa Knelman's was a feather on her calf muscle.

"You have to chill out, Spence." Chrys said as she pulled her brother off to the side away from the people filing out of the church. It had been a long time since she had seen him this angry about something she didn't do.

Spencer ran a hand through his hair, flattening some of the blond spikes. "This is all crazy though. Tessa would not have killed herself. Not the Tessa I know."

"You didn't know her that long, Spence, and that was over ten years ago. When was the last time you talked to her?" She saw his anger switch toward her and quickly added, "They had a full Catholic funeral, so that has to mean something."

"I guess." Spencer was nine when his family took in Chrys and it was shortly after that they stopped going to church every week and only went on holidays with other ventures into the Aboriginal world to give her some of her heritage. His dad seemed to lose his faith somewhere around that time. Spencer didn't know how strict the church still was on the "suicide as a sin" rule; however nobody in their right mind believed Tessa Knelman killed herself. How the hell did she end up hanging with an extension cord around her neck?

"Are we going to the reception?" Chrys nodded at the people crossing the street to the community center. She couldn't speak for him, but she was hungry. She was always hungry.

"I guess."

"We don't have to, you know." Chrys tugged down on the mid-length skirt to her tunic dress. She pulled up the sleeve to her elbow. The wind picked up suddenly and she forgot about the sleeve and reached up, but failed, to hold down her dark chestnut hair as it swirled around her head.

Spencer snatched his tie from the wind and tucked it inside his jacket. Just that sudden rapid movement caused a groan to slip through his lips. It wasn't long ago that he had been chained up, tortured and beaten. A bit of pain, as he called it, lingered.

"You're still hurting?"

"I'm fine."

"It's been two months and you're grunting like an old man. How is that fine?"

The parade of mourners crossed the street and entered the community center. They were in one of the small towns that was a forty-five minute drive outside Middleton. Most of the town was present plus more people who Tessa's smile had blessed in the city. A few people carried tripods and the large photos of Tessa that had been in the church.

Spencer and Tessa met in culinary school at the Culinary Institute of Canada across the country in Prince Edward Island and bonded because they were from the same city. They hadn't talked much since leaving school except on social media. She had always been the first one to give an encouraging word to anyone feeling down or to suggest something crazy on a day off. It was her idea for their group of friends to get tattoos. She was fun. She enjoyed life. Suicide wasn't her thing. It was impossible.

"Do you think I'd look good with a tattoo?"

"What?" Spencer had been thinking about his own tattoo experience and that he would have never done it without Tessa. Since then he'd had more tattoos and added a quote to the lobster. Had it not been for her perhaps he'd have none.

Chrys took her brother's silence as an opportunity to talk about something she cared about. "A tattoo. I want to get a tattoo."

"No way. You're not getting one."

"You have two, plus the quotes. That makes four tattoos."

"Chrys, can we talk about this later?"

"I don't even know why I'm asking you."

"Chrys!"

As soon as they were in the community center, Chrys found the tables of food contributed by restaurants Tessa had worked at in the city as well as women from the church. Her brother would have said she was pouting. Spencer found himself a bottle of pure glacial mountain water and started to wander through the room.

At the church, he'd recognized a few chefs, but none with whom he'd normally strike up a conversation. Tessa had apprenticed at the best high-end restaurants in the downtown area. These chefs hosted charity events and did cooking segments on Good Morning Middleton. They were the first to be contacted when Hollywood film crews were in town looking for caterers. He wasn't sure why Tessa ever left that high-end life, because they were the restaurants that could fast-track a chef into owning her own restaurant; going to work in a mountain resort was not. That was the type of place novice cooks went to bide their time and learn or veteran cooks went to, well, die. Spencer was the chef and owner of The Alcrest Gastropub, which he owned only because it was a family business and his father had died five years ago. He officially bought the restaurant from his mother two years after that. Sandra Bullock and Bradley Cooper would go to The Alcrest only if they were lost. The food was great, the atmosphere was relaxed; but he wasn't being featured in any magazines. Spencer gave a nod to one of the chefs he had imagined working with back when he was prepping food for his father and dreaming of something he thought was better.

Caroline Montgomery had been Tessa's best friend since she was six, if Spencer remembered correctly. He met her when she came to visit at culinary school and then she was sweet enough to drop by the restaurant to see him after he had moved back home and taken over. He had seen her at the front of the church. He watched her speak to a few people as she moved around. Her blond locks were short in a pixie cut. Her face was long. She gave half smiles to the people who talked to her, but her eyes showed her true emotions. She nervously flattened her maroon dress as people asked how she was doing.

Spencer sipped his water waiting until Caroline was alone for longer than thirty seconds. "Caroline, how have you been?"

"Thanks for coming, Spencer. I'm as good as can be expected." She ran a hand down over one hip smoothing out wrinkles in her dress that weren't there. "Have you talked to Tessa's parents?"

"No, I don't know if I ... I don't know. I don't know what to say. I wanted to talk to you first. Are they serious about the suicide?" Maybe he was being too blunt, but he was taking lessons from his little sister and not thinking before speaking.

"That's what the police up there said."

"Up where?"

"Where she was working. The Pass at Fontana Hot Springs. The RCMP officer there said his findings were that she..." Caroline looked around. When she finished her sentence she did so in a whisper, "killed herself." She shook her head without saying anything else.

"I read your post online. You don't think it was suicide."

"Of course not." Caroline faked a smile at someone expressing their condolences. "We've been friends since we were kids and living together off and on since she came back from culinary school ten years ago. She was a happy person. She loved life. Tessa wouldn't do that."

15

~ * ~

"The whole thing is bullshit," Caroline stated before taking a healthy drink of red wine. Spencer had asked her to The Alcrest after the gathering. They sat at a corner table away from most of the customers. There weren't that many anyway.

"So what do you think happened?" Spencer hadn't touched his drink yet. His jacket lay over the back of his chair. He had taken his tie off too, unbuttoned his collar and rolled up his sleeves. One of the scars left by his recent torture was still on his left forearm marking up the tattoo of a pig. That was going to be a constant reminder. He also had marks on both wrists from where he had been chained up. He was never comfortable in shirts and ties, but knew he looked good when he dressed up.

"I think she was murdered."

"Why do you think that?" Spencer had told his sister no more murder mysteries after their last involvement in one. They owned a restaurant and that was it. He was getting that tingling feeling, however, and couldn't help himself.

"She told me something strange was going on. She never gave me many details though. She said she didn't trust the people she worked with. Tessa wanted to come home, she said she was going to as soon as the summer was over, but said she had to find something out first. What does that sound like to you?"

His first thought was, not really much. "She didn't say what was going on?"

"She wanted to look into things farther to see if she was right before accusing anyone. She didn't tell me much. She was cryptic."

"What happened to her? Why do the police think it was suicide? I don't really know the details."

Caroline took a sip of her wine as she prepared herself to face what had happened. "She went missing August 3rd. According to the RCMP, because nobody else is talking to us, a security guard saw her at around 10:45pm walking with her knife kit on the road that goes by some old staff trailers that weren't used. She had to walk that road to get to her living quarters anyway, so it wasn't out of the ordinary. And you know how meticulous she was about her knives. She'd never leave them in the kitchen where any ass could use them. She was supposed to work in the morning, but didn't show up for her shift. Security went to her room to find her. Her roommate said Tessa didn't come back the night before. She thought maybe she'd gone to someone else's room. Tessa didn't have any love interests up there. She would have told me. Three days later they found her in one of the old staff trailers hanging by and extension cord from a beam in the ceiling." Caroline's breath caught as she tried to hold back tears. "They said there were a few knives laid out on a table and that she had cuts to her stomach, wrists and throat. Their theory is that she tried cutting and stabbing herself first, but the pain was too much and she decided to hang herself with whatever was there."

"That doesn't really sound like suicide to me. I know - knew, Tessa. She kept her knives razor sharp and wasn't afraid of pain. It wouldn't be hard for her to take herself out." One day in school Spencer had shown his friends what an old cook at the pub had him do when he started cooking. He had a pan on the heat with a touch of oil in it. The chefs put their fingertips down in the oil to see how long they could hold them there. Tessa had to prove she could beat the boys even though Spencer didn't really have any feeling in his fingertips left.

Caroline shrugged her shoulders. She had a couple years on Spencer's thirty-one with very few wrinkles or signs of age. "Other staff members there reported that she wasn't eating or sleeping and was keeping to herself. Her roommate said she found Tessa sharpening her knives in the bathroom at six in the morning a few days before she disappeared. I don't know why she would do that, but to them that means she was depressed and suicidal."

"What are we talking about?" Chrys curled one foot under her as she sat on a free chair. She had changed into grey yoga pants and a bright pink tank-top.

Spencer grunted. "That the cops think a chef who has razor sharp knives and probably a strong tolerance

18

for pain due to hundreds of on the job cuts and burns wimped out from cutting herself and changed her mind deciding to hang herself instead."

"Really? Statistically women prefer less violent ways like poison or drowning." Chrys got caught by her brother's glare. "What?"

"This was a woman who didn't flinch when she got her tattoo in PEI. She went through a cooking test with a third degree burn on her hand. She could handle pain."

"Was there a suicide note?"

Caroline shook her head. "They didn't find one. All recent texts were erased from her phone too, and when they sent her belongings home her mother said her journal was missing the last two weeks. She had kept a journal since I knew her, so she wouldn't just stop. There's a stack of them in her closet at our apartment going back to when she was little. She carried one everywhere and wrote in it every day and the same day she finished one journal she started another. She wrote what she was doing, dreams, plans, recipes…she wrote everything down."

"I remember that," Spencer said.

"The police say that the only thing that made sense was suicide. Nobody at the resort said anything about people not liking her or anything like that. She called me a couple weeks before and said someone left a note under her door telling her to watch what she was doing. Of course there was no note in her room and she didn't tell anyone else about it. There's no written record of it, so the police are saying I'm trying to make something where there was nothing. The police told me over the phone that without evidence it was hearsay and they had to go with solid evidence." Caroline finished her wine. She pushed the glass away keeping her fingers on the stem. "Nobody's listening to her parents or me. They say she killed herself and that's it. They won't do anything else until new evidence appears."

A large smile filled Chrys' pillowy lips. "Then we get some."

"No." Spencer stared at his sister. "Not you. I'm going."

"What?"

"Chrys, you're staying here. I'm going to send them a resume and see if I can get a job in their kitchen. I'll snoop around and see what …"

"How the monkey-fuck are you going to do that? Spencer Alcrest may not be famous, but one call and they can find out who you are." Chrys didn't notice her brother's friend flinch at her wild vocabulary.

"So?"

"So, dear brother, isn't it going to be suspicious if someone who owns his own restaurant is looking for a job at some mountain resort? Unless you're going to change your name."

Caroline was quiet as the two went back and forth developing a plan from a name change to who could give him a reference. After a few minutes she said, "Tessa needs justice, but not at risking your lives."

"I'll get the job, look around for a few days and get out. I'll be up there a week, tops."

"Assuming you can get a job." Chrys noted.

Spencer raised an eyebrow. He knew what chefs looked for in resumes. He had hired a few cooks because of excellent resumes and got burned when they barely knew what end of the French knife to hold. He could probably get any chef anywhere to take a look at his resume and give him a call. Whether or not he could find out if a suicide was actually homicide was the true question. If he could do it without being hung himself was the challenge.

Chapter 2

"I thought your brother wasn't going to let you get a tattoo."

Chrys hid the smile on her face in the headrest of the chair – so glad she was sitting backward in it - at the way the Australian woman pronounced tattoo, "tadoo." She winced and groaned as the needles touched the back of her shoulder. She tried focusing on the woman's artwork on the wall and controlling any reaction to the pain. The outline was almost done. Every touch of the needles seared into her skin. "I'm twenty-six. He's just my brother. I can do what I want. Besides, I put him on a bus this morning. Oh fay-fay duh pee-yen that hurts."

"What the hell was that?"

"Ever see the show Firefly?"

Sloane's red-lipped smile lit up her entire face. Chrys was in trouble. "Can't say that I have." She claimed to have over thirty tattoos on her body and Chrys wanted to see them all.

From the apartment she shared with her brother above the restaurant, Chrys had watched her reading a book on the bench outside the tattoo shop every day around lunch time. After a week of walking the dogs at the same time every day she crossed the street to introduce herself.

"We'll have to watch it some time."

"It's a date." The woman wiped away excess ink and dove back into the tattoo. They said getting a tattoo was like running a fingernail over a bad sunburn. As far as Chrys was concerned they were full of shit. It was more like drawing a picture deep in the skin with a dull pointed knife with rust on it. "Where's your bro off to?"

"Off to be a big damn hero." Chrys told her about what had happened to her brother's friend and how he was adamant that she didn't commit suicide. It had taken almost two weeks, but now he was on a thirteen-hour bus ride into the Rocky Mountains to start a job as a sous chef at The Pass at Fontana Hot Springs. "He hopes to solve her murder."

"By himself? I thought you two were a detective team like Starsky and Hutch."

"I guess, but this time Spence wants to go solo. Idiot's going to get himself hurt." She winced as the needles dug in.

"So don't let him. There's got to be some investigating you can do around here. You told me about her funeral and all that. Maybe you can find out about her life. Maybe she was depressed. Maybe it was suicide and your bro is wasting his time."

Chrys had dated both sexes, but after an encounter with a drag performer and the fallout from that she swore off men. This woman made her nervous. She never got nervous about relationships. Of course they weren't in one, they were just friends. Being topless hanging onto the back of a chair while Sloane's hands were all over her bare shoulder gave Chrys all sorts of tingles in her belly.

"I can do that," Chrys said as she grit her teeth. "It can't hurt right."

~ * ~

Chrys rolled her shoulder as she waited for someone to open the door. Even wearing capris and a plaid shirt (sleeves rolled to the elbows and only two buttons fastened) she was still perspiring beneath the sun. The sweat got under her wrapped artwork and made it sting. The door opened and she instantly tried to control her twitching.

"Can I help you?" It took a moment for Caroline to recognize the younger woman. "Chrys, right? Is Spencer with you?"

"No, he's not. Right now, he's on his way up to Fontana."

"He's actually going? I didn't know if he would."

"Yeah he is. I was hoping I could talk to you about her. I don't really know much about Tessa." She saw the woman barely nod. "You said she had been your roommate for ten years?"

Caroline's grey eyes dropped. "Off and on depending on where she was working and if I was in a relationship or not. More often not. She left for The Pass four months before," Caroline held her breath a moment, "before she died. I'm sorry. It still gets to me. She took care of my son when I worked and cooked for us. We were her guinea pigs for new dishes."

"I didn't know you were a mom."

"I have an eight year old son. He's in school right now."

Being face to face with her Chrys wasn't sure what she was doing there or what she should be asking. What would she want someone to ask if she were killed? "You said you still have some of her stuff here."

"I do. Why?"

Saying she wanted to see if this woman was secretly suicidal wasn't going to win any prizes. "I know my brother said he wanted to do this alone, but I'd still like to know who he's doing it for. That make sense? I only met Tessa once at their graduation. If my brother's life is on the line I'd like to know for whom."

"Do you really think his life is at risk?"

"You tell me. How serious was Tessa when she told you something suspicious was going on?"

"Come in." Caroline led the way into her two-story house. There was a stack of realtor signs leaning on the wall with her photo and name on them. The stairs that went up had toys pushed to one side of nearly every step. Her son was into trucks. Photographs on the wall were of a young boy at different stages of growing up. There were no photos of a man and few of the woman leading the way. The further up the stairs they got Tessa showed up in some of the photos. Again she was smiling. "Can I get you something to drink?"

"No, that's okay. Am I keeping you from something?"

"I have to meet someone to show a house, but I have some time. Have a seat." They were now in a large kitchen with a small dining table beneath a window. The remnants of a Lego village were on one side of the table built over a book with a colourful waterfall on the cover. The water was a green kaleidoscope. She crossed to the kitchen counter and came back with a stack of handwritten letters that she held out. "Tessa was old school. She sent these and wrote with pen in her journals…"

"Are those here? The journals?" Chrys' eyes were wide. She ground her teeth as her shoulder touched the high backed chair.

"They are. I told her parents I would get her journals to them, but I've been busy." She didn't sit down. Instead she turned to the refrigerator and started straightening fruit magnets. "That's not true. I can't bring myself to go into her room. I've tried and I just start bawling."

"So Tessa wrote these letters to you?"

Caroline hummed. "One a week. We texted almost every day when she could get service, however, she still wrote me a letter once a week telling me what was going on there. You can read them if you want. She talks about the beauty of the mountains and her hikes and her job. I didn't see anything out of the ordinary."

Chrys flipped through the letters not really looking for anything. The handwriting was neat with round loops and straight lines, much neater than her own. "Did she write anything about being depressed?"

"No. She said she was lonely a few times and wasn't really making friends up there, but nothing about being sad or anything. Tessa always said suicide was a purely selfish act. She'd never do that to her parents."

"What about whatever she thought was going on up there? You said she was worried about something."

Caroline moved to the far side of the table. With manicured fingers she pushed away some of the Lego pieces from the edge. "She said it was feelings she had, something like that. She was uncomfortable I guess. Most of what she told me was over the phone, so there's no record of it."

Of course it was, Chrys thought.

"She did write in the last letter that she was uneasy and thought she was being watched. You can read it there. The last time she called she did it from a payphone because she thought they were listening to her conversations somehow. I told her she was getting paranoid and told her she needed to come home and get a job here. She could have any job in any kitchen she wanted."

"When was that?"

"Almost two weeks before she died."

"Why did she go work at the resort? Spencer said Tessa had been working at Terre Rouge the last he heard. He didn't even know she had switched jobs until her death."

"Tessa was her own person. She did things on a whim all the time. One day she told me she had a job up there and was on a bus the next day."

"That was normal for her?" From what her brother had told her, Chrys knew that a chef had to be strategic with their careers. It wasn't a simple matter of taking any job. If you wanted to be the best you had to plan ahead.

Caroline shrugged her shoulders. "She liked adventure."

"Can I keep these letters? I'll make sure you get them back." Chrys gave a half smile as the phone in her pocket started to sing. It was the restaurant's ring tone. Someone called in sick and they want her to serve. She waited until it stopped. Normally she stored the phone in her bra, but thanks to the tattoo she wasn't wearing one today. "Can I see her room?"

Caroline checked the time on a thin wristwatch before agreeing. "Her room's upstairs. So, you and Spencer are brother and sister?" The question had been asked before. It was people's way of trying to end their curiosity about Spencer Alcrest being Caucasian and Chrys Alcrest being Aboriginal.

"My mom disappeared or flaked off when I was three, so I went into the foster system and the Alcrests took me in. I guess for some reason they liked me because they kept me for a while."

"I didn't mean to pry. I just figured since you were asking questions about Tessa I could ask questions about you."

As Chrys followed her up the stairs, she caught a glimpse of the woman's behind in her tight slacks. She was dressed in a very nice business suit that would put any home buyer at ease. "So what's your theory about Tessa?"

Without turning it, Caroline wrapped her fingers around a doorknob. "Maybe she saw something she shouldn't have. I heard of someone getting killed in the Philippines for turning in employees for stealing from the kitchen. A lot of rich people go up to the hot springs, so who knows who's up there. I really don't know. Maybe she did kill herself. She wouldn't though. I don't know." She wiped a tear from her cheek then opened the bedroom door and stepped aside.

The bedroom was spotless. It smelled musty. The bed was made with a colourful striped comforter on top. The other furnishings were extremely simple. There was a dresser with a collection of framed photographs covering the entire top - Tessa in culinary school, at the beach, in New York, on a mountain cliff, in the wood - always smiling and happy. Could she have been hiding pain? On the wall beside the bed was the same culinary degree certificate that Spencer had in his office at the restaurant. Clothes weren't tossed around like in Chrys' bedroom. She took a close look at a small vanity with a tiny assortment of make-up on it. There was a layer of dust on everything.

"Tessa didn't use much make-up, eye shadow and lipstick mostly. She didn't paint her fingernails because of her job."

"Was she always this tidy?"

"Not always. Look, I have to go and meet my clients."

"Can I see Tessa's notebooks?"

"They're in her closet. I really have to leave though."

Chrys opened the closet's folding doors. A good amount of clothes hung from the rod with few empty spaces. The chef jackets from the Culinary Institute of Canada were there. Her shoes were simple with modest heels. This was the complete opposite of her own closet. On the shelf above her head were a couple of cardboard boxes with notebooks showing out over the top. "Chrys, please."

"Can I take them with me? I promise I'll return them in perfect condition." Chrys already had one box half-way off the shelf.

"Take them. Her parents have the one that was sent to them after her death, but like I said it was missing the last couple of weeks. I might be able to get it for you to read. I really have to get going though." Caroline walked away from the door and down the hallway.

With a tug Chrys had the box above her head. She slowly let it down until it was cradled in her arms. Inside were over a dozen books. All were the same size with solid red covers. Corners of loose papers showed. She quickly fingered a couple of the books and saw that they were the most recent. The latest book was six months ago. She put the letters on top and left the room, carefully closing the door behind her.

It was looking like Tessa Knelman had always been a happy person. Judging from her photos, she liked to experience life. Killing herself didn't seem to be an option. That meant her brother was going into something else, something unknown. And if his friend didn't kill herself then he was going to a place where someone got away with murder.

Chapter 3

With eyes closed Spencer worked the kinks out of his neck. If he had driven to Fontana it would have taken him nine hours. Instead he caught a Greyhound bus and had just rounded hour thirteen up into the Canadian Rocky Mountains. Every town they came to demanded a fifteen-minute stop to wait for passengers to enter or exit and freight to be unloaded. In one town they had to wait forty-five minutes for another bus to meet them. The air smelled of diesel fuel and sweat. He was tired of hearing the muffled music from people's headphones and the wild assortment of noises that came from people's bodies. If he heard the guy three seats back cough up a phlegm ball one more time there would be more than Tessa's murder on his hands. Luckily the farting lady got off the bus an hour ago.

The bus drove through the small village of Fontana without stopping. Instead Spencer had to get off the bus sixteen kilometers down the highway at Kenora.

Night had dropped amid the mountain ranges. Now, after 10:30 pm the only light was on a pole outside a roadside building. During the day it had a restaurant, convenience store and post office, however everything was closed by 8:00 pm. All he saw now was the single lightbulb on a curved pole out front of the store above a bench made of varnished logs. The "village" of Kenora barely ranked a spot on a map.

The moment the bus drove away, Spencer checked his phone. The signal indicator showed only one bar. A text might get through, but a phone call would crack and probably get lost. What if someone knew he was a fake? Luring him up in the mountains on a back highway where all phone service was sketchy at best was a good plan.

"I'm starting to think like Chrys."

Ten minutes passed before he saw a pair of headlights coming the same way the bus had come. His right hand gripped his backpack, the left rested just inside the open zipper. His Superior Culinary Master 10" French knife was just inside. It was a heavy knife he had since culinary school made of high carbon surgical steel with full tang. He sharpened it the night before he left.

Time to see if his ruse worked.

The white SUV pulled into the parking lot in front of the store and circled so the driver's side was next to him. The door read *The Pass at Fontana Hot Springs*

Resort with the picture of a winding path through mountains. Maybe it was a river.

"Spencer Hart?" The face of an older gentleman smiled out at him through an open window.

"That's me," Spencer responded with a smile and nod. He threw his suitcase into the back seat and climbed into the front placing his backpack between his feet on the floor. "It gets pretty quiet up here."

"Everything shuts down before dark. Only places open in Fontana are the resort lounge and the bar in town. Some nights it's just the lounge."

"So there is a town? I didn't really see anything when we drove by."

The guard laughed. "No, we call it town, but it's basically a strip mall with a half dozen or so stores. They have what you need." His grey hair curled from under a baseball cap.

"What's your name?"

"Stanley. I read a book once with a detective named Jake Hart. Any relation?" He had one of those bellowing laughs that was funnier than the joke.

"I don't think so. How long have you worked at the resort?"

"Five years. I retired out here six years ago and started working for them a year later. Can't stand sitting around."

Spencer checked the service on his phone. It hadn't improved much. "So, people actually live out here year-round?"

"Oh yeah. It takes a certain kind of person to stay out here, that's for sure. Fontana probably has about four hundred people. All the seasonal workers, campers and tourists are on top of that."

"That have anything to do with that girl I read about? The isolation, I mean." Spencer held his breath. He didn't mean to bring the subject of Tessa up, but couldn't help himself.

"Some people can't handle the solitude out here. I never met her, but was told she was depressed and lonely. Some kids get up here and leave after two weeks. You just make sure you talk to people and don't be alone and you'll be fine."

Stanley turned off the highway and drove up a hill sparsely lit by street lamps. Halfway up Spencer saw houses on the left, with many of the windows lit. Another road cut off to the right. He got a glimpse at a sign reading Model Home. He wondered what everything would look like during the daylight. Right now there were stars above and then dark voids where the sky must meet mountain. The SUV turned a corner at the top of a hill and the head-lights revealed a horse paddock. A few of the beasts looked out at the intruder. Beyond that a three-story lodge building. In the dark it blended into the mountains and trees; only its windows, now lit up, revealed its size and shape.

"Here you go. If I were you I'd keep any questions you have about that incident to yourself. Do your job and don't get lonely. That's all there is to it." The old man gave him a smile.

Tonight Spencer was staying in the main lodge. He called his sister on the room phone and told her he was okay. She said The Alcrest was fine and nothing interesting had happened. As he hung up the phone with her he dialed his girlfriend's number. Jesse was also the front-of-house manager at the restaurant. They didn't have the best relationship; however, he still felt the need to call her.

Ten minutes later he turned off the lights. Tomorrow he would find out about his kitchen and move to the staff quarters. Tomorrow he would start finding suspects. Tomorrow was the day.

~ * ~

The main floor of the lodge was, when you got down to it, open concept with weight bearing walls put in place to create the illusion of wide corridors. In the center was the Springs Lounge with glass doors opening onto the hot spring pools. Behind one of the walls was the Valley View Dining Room. It offered fine dining cuisine while the lounge served burgers and fries. Both, as far as he could tell, were fed by the same kitchen. He took a quick peek into both before reaching the front desk.

"Excuse me. I'm supposed to meet the chef."

"You're the new sous chef." The woman behind the front desk smiled the brightest good-morning smile she could muster. Her teeth were dazzling white. "We've been waiting for you."

Spencer stared at her for a moment. Waiting for him how? Waiting to string him up? Waiting to play games with him?

"We're so glad you're here."

He heard a "ting" and saw a glint of light when she smiled. He couldn't deal with perky without a cup of coffee. "I don't know how to get in touch with the chef."

"I can radio him for you. All the important people carry two-way radios." She smiled again. This one was a, *I will do whatever I can to fulfill your needs,* kind of smile. She wore the company's maroon and silver golf shirt. Her shoulder-length brown hair matched the company colours with maroon streaks on either side - the Fontana poster child.

"You're the new sous chef for Northview Golf Course?" The other person behind the desk was a man with Asian eyes, a pearl-white smile, and hair that flowed in black waves. Even when he wasn't moving the collar-length locks looked like black liquid. He smelled of fancy cologne (something too expensive for the cook to ever consider) and was also in a great mood. "The food is great down there, but they could really use someone in charge."

"Why don't they have anyone?"

"Kitchen staff got moved around when …" the smile slipped for just a second "… ah when another sous chef left the restaurant up here. What's your name, by the way? I'm Tony and this is Blaire." Bright smile. Spencer wondered if bright teeth was a pre-requisite for front desk staff.

Tessa left? Was that how they were describing it?

"Where did you work before coming here?"

"For Chef Garrett Mecredi at Legend Restaurant in Middleton. That was my last job." Garrett had graduated with Spencer and Tessa. He was in that tattoo photo with the two of them. He was now one of those hoity-toyties that were too good for him. He said there was no problem giving a reference if someone called.

"A superstar chef then." Tony's face had to hurt from all the smiling.

"I'm okay."

"I radioed Chef." Blaire wiggled the hand-held two-way radio. Her smile this time indicated, mission accomplished. "He'll be up here to meet you as soon as he can. Please have a seat while you wait."

From his expensive leather chair, he watched people walking the corridors. There were a few meeting rooms of different sizes around the restaurant areas. He could see through a glass wall into a small store with resort collector items and a few supplies. At the end of the corridor was a spa offering pedicures, manicures, massages and all sorts of treatments. A

41

sign displayed the prices. He couldn't understand why someone would pay so much to have their face covered in mud.

A man in black pants with thin white pinstripes and a white chef coat stopped at the front desk. He didn't seem much older than Spencer. He was thin and tall like him, with short hair and trimmed beard, both the colour of rust on an old car. He slapped one of the walkie-talkie against his thigh. "Spencer? Sorry to make you wait. I'm Chef Sam King."

Spencer remembered a joke he saw on Facebook about how the Dementors in Harry Potter didn't go after the red-headed Ron Weasley because he didn't have a soul. Maybe red-heads didn't have souls. Perhaps this was the one who'd strung up Tessa.

When he smiled his upper lip crept up exposing skull formed gums. "Are you ready? I'll give you a tour and take you to your restaurant."

"I'm not working here?" (Tessa had worked at the main lodge.)

"We have five restaurants here. Two are in the lodge plus the staff cafeteria. Then one at each golf course, but each of those does two different types of menus. You'll be the sous chef of the kitchen at Northview Golf Course, but since I'm so spread out you're basically the chef. You do the ordering and deal with the staff. For all intensive purposes you are the chef." He smiled again and Spencer was sure he could see his actual skull through the man's gums.

42

Without much warning the mountains seemed to grow behind the lodge building. They rose quickly covered in green pines and spruce with black cliffs covered in white caps above them. Turning around he could see the valley. He knew there was a river cutting through the trees and greenery down there. On the far side of the valley more mountains rose circling in the whole thing. They too had white caps. Jagged points arose like different layers of an animals teeth. It was much nicer in daylight.

"Up above are the Indian tubs," Chef Sam continued. He pointed to a rectangle building of tan rock and clay with three open windows on a flat rock outcrop behind a row of trees. "They were made by the first people who came here. Did you get to try the hot spring pools?"

"Not yet. I got in late."

"You really should. One of the perks is you get to use them for free. You can also sign out an ATV four-wheeler and go golfing on your days off."

His tour was quick. Spencer didn't have time to memorize where things were. Behind the lodge, past the closed off road leading to the ski slopes, was one of several RV parks. Most overnight visitors brought their own accommodations. Half-way down the hill to the highway was where most of the year round population lived. It was the area where he'd seen lights last night. There were homes in the area of The Valley Golf Course, but those were mostly timeshare houses and condominiums. The "town" had a grocery store, bank, sub shop, a Greek restaurant that only stayed busy thanks to pizza sales, the bar and a small store which sold a wider range of collectables than the one in the lodge. Across the highway in The Valley area most of the buildings had a red and white paint scheme with clay shingled roofs like a tropical villa. The club house looked the same. New houses were being built and all would look similar.

"You a golfer? This course has a lot of water hazards. The other course has more trees and long drives. Both are good courses though."

"I've only golfed once or twice. I'm just here to work."

"They have rental clubs. You get one day off through the week, sometimes two if you're lucky. There are hiking trails and you usually can find a ride into Yanko. It's an hour away, but it's the closest town to us."

Almost a kilometer down the highway from the main town the truck crossed from the golf course to an RV park that had one long two story building right at the front. At one time it had been a motel called Birch Grove Motel, but the owners of the resort bought it and changed it to staff accommodations. Chef Sam parked the truck in front. All around it were recreational campers. As he stepped from the truck he heard kids screaming at each other, someone banging on something and the sounds of the river which circled the park splashing over rocks. The odor of a campfire was in the air.

"Here's your new home. Pretty basic rooms. You have your own bathroom, which is nice. I believe you don't have a roommate at the moment. That can always change though. Men are on the first floor and women on the second with a shared kitchen, lounge and laundry room. You have Wifi too, but I don't know how good it is."

"Are there other accommodations?" Spencer wasn't sure where Tess had been staying. He knew she had a roommate, but not where she was living.

"There is another building, sort of like an apartment building, above the town where staff stays, but we don't have any openings. Everyone wants to live closer to town and the lodge. We haven't had an opening there since the summer started."

After dropping his suitcase in his room they got in the truck and continued the tour. Spencer said nothing and just nodded his head. He wasn't getting bad feelings from this man. Did that really mean anything? How many people out there never knew their polite neighbor was a killer?

Across the river and up onto the hill were more houses built amid the forest. They ran up the mountainside along perfectly manicured fairways.

"These houses are owned by people from Calgary and Middleton. A lot are lived in year round, but some are just holiday houses. The owner of the resort has one."

The Northview clubhouse was a rectangular building with a glass wall and deck facing the first green. The colour scheme was more natural than that in the valley. There were a lot of dark browns. The mountain seemed to rise up without warning with the course circling around it.

Chef Sam parked the truck. "That barn there," a tall weathered building that looked ready to fall, "dates back to the 1800's and the first settlers in the area. It's been fortified, but I still tell people to stay away from it. And those trailers over there are the old staff trailers. Stay away from them too." There were three long mobile-home trailers. Grass grew up around the outsides making them look like they were potted there.

"That's where she was found," Spencer said without thinking.

"What?"

"What?" Spencer repeated. This was his sister's thing. She put herself in these situations and he got her out. "I read about a girl who … she did whatever …"

"You mean Tessa Knelman?" He drummed his fingers on the steering wheel as he stared across to the beige trailers. His eyes were actually caring. Spencer didn't expect that. "That was something tragic that will hopefully not happen again. I keep telling the head office we should get those trailers taken out of here. They haven't been used since last summer and I think everything usable has been stripped from them." He walked around the front of the truck and met Spencer by his door. "They left desks and chairs and some small televisions in there, so everybody took what they wanted for their rooms."

"Guess I'm too late." Spencer smiled showing his dimples.

"Yeah, I'll call the maintenance guys as soon as we're done and see if we can get rid of them. We don't need that hanging over us."

"I guess not," Spencer said. He had to get in there. He had to see where his friend died. He knew there probably weren't any clues that had been missed, but he had to see it for himself. As he followed the chef through the back door to the Northview clubhouse Spencer couldn't help taking another look at the trailers.

"Everybody come on over." There were only three staff in the kitchen. Chef Sam quickly introduced Spencer and listed a few of his fake credentials. "He's your sous chef, so he's in charge. This is Amam, your chef d'partie. He's your second in command. He's been taking care of things down here after we moved Jacob up to the main a few weeks ago, so he'll show you what to do. This is Stuart, your breakfast and lunch cook and this is Bobbi. She's doing prep and dishes now, but we're training her as a cook."

At the last statement Spencer saw something between the co-workers. Bobbi dropped her eyes and pursed her lips. Amam turned away. Spencer was willing to bet the dark-skinned man – who had a thick accent when he welcomed the new comer – was from a country where women were not thought of highly in the workplace.

"How's it going?" Stuart put his fist out and waited to have it bumped. His sandy hair overflowed from beneath a company baseball cap. He had that stoner, surfer vibe that Spencer's own sous chef had. Only this guy was tall (a few inches past six feet) and so thin he reminded Spencer of an 80's hairband rocker.

"Good. A lot of stuff to take in all in one day."

"It gets easier." Stuart had a Joker smile, the Heath Ledger one, not Jack Nicholson. "I've been here six months and know where everything is, so if you need anything just ask."

"I've lived here four years," Bobbi stated. She was the opposite of Stuart in that she was short and stout. She wore a white beanie cap over pulled-back hair. The cuffs on her chef jacket and checked pants were rolled up. She became quiet when all eyes turned to her.

Chef Sam said, "You'll meet your other breakfast cook Wednesday morning. Kevin and Stuart switch up every week."

"I love having Wednesday off. Karaoke at the bar Tuesday night, bro." Stuart stuck his tongue out.

"That's why we do it that way," the Chef said. "Spencer has orientation the rest of the day then you'll start tomorrow at 10:00 am. That good?"

As they left, Spencer nodded to Amam, but the man barely tilted his head. Was he pissed off at being pushed out of the head job or was he just a prick? Spencer didn't want to trust any of them. Anyone who worked at Fontana could have had a hand in his friend's death. Certainly a few were involved in covering it up. He wished his sister were here. She'd have some ideas of what to do and crazy plans to get it done.

Step one was orientation, which included lunch in the cafeteria and hopefully getting to know more staff. Step two, visit the crime scene. Step three, was to not get killed. Easy.

Chapter 4

"Can I help you?"

"Coffee," Spencer blurted out as he spun around. A woman was standing behind him and he'd just been caught doing something he shouldn't. He had opened every cupboard door of the community kitchen at Birch Grove. It was on the second floor and below it was the shared lounge. "Can anybody use the coffee or does someone own it?"

"It's for everyone," she said blankly as she crossed from the hallway to the microwave with a styrophome cup of instant noodles in her hands. She had sun-bleached highlights in chestnut hair and freckles on each cheekbone. She was pretty, but looked cold.

Spencer had managed to stay awake during an orientation presentation for himself and nine other new staff. He found the history interesting – the name Fontana Pass went back to the first settlers to make their way across the mountains – and hearing about the parts of the lodge somewhat useful, but he was still tired from the bus trip. He had a crime scene to investigate. He wasn't sure what the nightlife was here or what the specific hours of work were. His restaurant at the golf course closed at 10:00 pm, so he couldn't investigate the old staff trailers until after that and after everyone was gone. Clean down of the kitchen and dining room was probably a half hour. If staff lived down here that was another fifteen minutes walking where the sun fell behind the mountains and set early every night.

"Have you worked here long?" he asked as he measured the coffee.

"Since the start of summer." She kept her back to him.

"You like it here? I'm Spencer, by the way."

"Louise." She added water to her noodles and set the microwave timer. "It's okay." That wasn't one of the phrases used in their recruitment. They said it was a wonderful place to work – "amazing" was the word used a couple times. Nowhere in the orientation did they say the lodge or area was okay.

"What do you do?"

"I'm a beer-cart girl. I drive around The Valley Golf Course selling beer to golfers." She didn't sound that excited about it. Her voice was rather flat.

Spencer was hoping to get a feel for things. "Must be good tips, eh?"

"Sometimes." As soon as the timer was done she took her cup of noodles and escaped down the hallway.

During orientation at the lodge the staff seemed happier. Those presenting it wore painted-on smiles as they talked about hiking trails and natural beauty. Maybe Fontana was not such a happy place.

Back in his room he checked the messages on his phone. They did have WiFi at Birch Grove; however, the more staff that came back to their rooms the more the signal got stretched. If people in the RV Park hitchhiked on it getting online was like pissing into a bottle in the dark – you might get lucky once in a while, but chances were you would just piss all over the place. That was one of his dad's sayings. His sister had texted a few times. She sent pictures of the dogs to prove they were okay. Another one said she might be in love. Most asked what was going on and why he wasn't texting back. Jessie texted a report on how business was going. Hanni, a server, reminded him she had requested a weekend off. He texted back to remind Jessie since she was in charge. His sous chef, Gordie, sent a message that Chrys was being bossy. He replied that she was the boss. This wasn't going to be easy. Nobody ever told him that owning your own business and being a chef meant running a daycare. When his father ran the business Spencer saw the practical jokes the cooks played on each other. He didn't realize how much it happened or how much the staff tried to get away with. And his sister was usually the whiniest brat of them all. Now she was in charge of The Alcrest.

"Why are you pissing Gordie off?" Spencer said the moment his sister answered the phone.

"What? How am I … I didn't. Hello to you too." Chrys rubbed her shoulder against the back of the couch. Her brother's bulldog lay at her feet while her Chihuahua, Breeze, was cuddled as close to her leg that it could get. "How's it going up there?"

"It's okay. I haven't done anything yet." Spencer's room was just a typical motel room. It had two beds with a small bedside table between them. Two dressers lined one wall with a television as close to the middle as it could be placed. The artwork on the wall featured, of course, mountain scapes. He was pretty sure when he was a kid he had stayed in dozens of motel rooms that looked exactly the same, right down to the worn down carpet.

"Have you met Louise Chambers yet?" Chrys suddenly asked.

"Who's that?"

"Tessa's roommate. You have to find her and get her to talk. I think she's the key."

Spencer wasn't sure if the Louise he met was the one his sister was talking about, but he didn't want to tell her either. "Chrys, I told you to stay out of this. I can handle it." He paced back and forth across the room.

"But Spence…"

"How did you get her name anyway?" He stood in front of the window looking down at the RVs parked behind the building. Some must have been lifelong campers because outside the door of their RV was a wood deck or covered carpark. Some looked better than actual houses.

"Get down Breeze. I got it from her letters to Caroline."

"How the hell did you do that?" His voice went up a few octaves. "When did you get letters from Caroline?"

Chrys tried scratching the back of her shoulder with her bottle of water. "Bro, it doesn't matter how I got the letters. I just got them. Someone has to do something."

"I'm up in the frigging Rockies, Chrys. I can't do more than what I'm doing." He closed the shade. "I have to go, Chrys. I have some more nothing to do." He pressed the off button and tossed his phone onto the bed. Five minutes later he got a text from her telling him to be careful.

~ * ~

When Spencer left the motel there was nobody around. He had heard others in the hallway coming and going from their rooms. Doors opened and closed. There were voices of people talking and laughing as they got back from wherever they had been, but as he left his room they all seemed to have disappeared. It made him leave later than he planned. Outside there were only a few vehicles close to the building. Not many employees actually had their own vehicles. He put his earbuds in without turning on the music. A car sped down the highway as he walked across the bridge. If they noticed him at all he was just someone out for a walk and listening to tunes. He kept the phone in his hand with the flashlight on.

Fontana was black again. There were lamps along the road across the highway winding around The Valley Golf Course. The mountains had vanished into the night sky. It was strange there. It was as if he could feel the tall beasts looming over him, circling him.

Across the bridge he took the side road that began rising instantly. The houses along the road mostly looked expensive. There were no rusting cars with flat tires and tall grass growing around them like the ones Spencer saw at the homes of childhood friends. One brown house at a corner had a deck from the second floor to the second floor of a garage. He had never seen anything like that before. Spencer didn't think he would ever own a house like that. His family had owned the restaurant and lived in a small house down the street. For a few summers during Spencer's teens his father needed to get his mind out of the restaurant, so he purchased houses in the rural area and fixed them up before reselling them. None of them had ever been as nice as those he was seeing on the side of the mountain.

There were no street lights except at each corner. He turned his flashlight off and walked by the feel of the road beneath his shoes. He tried keeping one foot on the paved road and the other in the grass along the edge. Light from living-room windows shone out helping him move along. His ears scanned the area listening for animals or the sounds of vehicles. He wasn't sure what he would do if he encountered an animal or a vehicle. As he got close to the Northview parking lot there were more street lights. To get to the trailers he had to go through them.

It took almost thirty minutes to walk from the motel to the clubhouse. A few times he stepped completely off the paved road onto the grass shoulder and stumbled. Spencer went right to the back door of the restaurant. If anyone was around he could say he was practicing the walk. The old barn stood as a black wall just outside the light. His aquamarine eyes stared in the direction of the trailers struggling to see what was out there. He held up his hand, blocking the light from above him, and could see the black rectangles of the old staff quarters. He didn't know much about them. They could have been locked for all he knew and didn't know which one contained the murder scene. Maybe he should have planned this better.

His phone vibrated in his hand. His eyes moved. No, something else moved. He stared across to the trailers. All he saw were dark shapes; he couldn't see definition in anything. Something had moved. He took one earbud out and strained to hear. A truck went by on the highway, there was a bird somewhere, moths bounced off the light above him. Was somebody watching him? He was in the bright light – exposed.

As Spencer started to walk again he let the earbud swing over his chest and shoved his hands in his pockets. He headed up the road that led from the old staff trailers to a couple of maintenance sheds. Beyond them was the road he had seen last night with the Model Home sign at the end. Somewhere on the far side was a footpath leading to the lodge. That would have been the path Tessa took every day – the one where she was last seen.

He felt sweat run down his back under his black hooded sweatshirt. He wore that (with the hood up) and black chef pants. His face pointed forward, but his eyes looked to the left. He felt the perspiration on his face and neck. It cooled the moment it came through his pores and was touched by the night air. The pavement ended just outside the light circle and his running shoes crunched on gravel. He almost stumbled in a pothole.

Something moved.

Spencer stopped. The movement had been right by the trailers. Whoever it was, they were short and moved slowly. Somebody crouched over perhaps. And silent. There had been no sound at all. He held his breath. The muscles in his legs started to quake. Tessa had died in there.

It moved again, no, walked. Thin legs…four legs. Deer. His eyes had adjusted enough to the dark to see the deer grazing on the grass in front of the trailers. There were least four of them. In orientation he'd learned there were a lot of deer were on the property. Mountain lions and bear stayed further up in the mountains.

He took a dozen more steps before getting off the road onto the grass. The night moisture instantly soaked into his running shoes. The deer looked in his direction with little care. They went back to munching grass while keeping their eyes on him.

Spencer sensed the shape of three long trailers. He had been in ones like these. They probably had a dozen rooms in each with a shared bathroom at one end. Something caught in his chest. He shouldn't be there. He saw the roof lights of a transport truck go down the highway and through the trees. The sound of its engine barely made it to him. Where he stood he couldn't see any lights except that of Northview and some down in the valley. Even looking up he couldn't see the lodge. This would be the perfect place to kill someone. There was nobody around. Trees and mountains muffled any sounds. There were roadways for escape. After the restaurant closed nobody would be in the area until 7:00 am. Almost ideal. It had worked at least once. Someone could kill him right there, right now and be in Alberta before the body was discovered. Hide the body and they could cross the border into the United States and be sipping shitty beer watching a baseball game without a worry in the world.

A leaf fluttered somewhere between the second and third trailers. Spencer stepped between the two and pressed a button on his cell phone to wake the home screen. There were six text messages waiting to be read. He'd look at those later. He quickly found the flashlight app and turned it on. Light erupted from the back of the device. He held it to his chest snuffing out the light and quickly looked around again. He couldn't see anyone; he couldn't even see the deer any more. They were on the other side. His heart pounded. Yellow police tape danced in the light breeze.

Chrys wouldn't hesitate.

Spencer ducked under the police tape. He probed the ground with his light. All of the grass had been trampled.

A wooded deck connected the two trailers. A door on each side led into each trailer. The one on the right previously had police tape across it. One end fluttered free in the wind.

Someone had been in there after the police. The killers cleaning up or someone wanting to see? Tessa's ghost?

Spencer tried the door handle. It wasn't locked. The hinges squealed. His light showed he was in a hallway that went the length of the trailer with doors along one side and windows on the side facing the other trailer. A black rubber mat covered the floor. The air was stale. He didn't like being in there. He couldn't hear anything. All sounds from the outside were gone and nothing inside made any noise. If it did he'd shit his pants. He looked down one way with his light. As he turned the other way the shadows seemed to stretch. They reached out for him. It was all in his head, but knowing that didn't make it any easier. His breath came fast. He hated the dark. Bad things happened in the dark.

He opened the first door. Inside was the frame of a bed and a desk. The chair was missing. There were curtains covering the window. There was nothing outstanding at all; nothing stood out.

The flashlight turned off. The front of his phone lit up with his sister's face looking up at him. He fought the sudden urge to crouch down low. He answered, but didn't say a word.

"Spencer?" The voice came out of the speaker like a grinding pain in his neck. "Helllloooooo?"

"What?" He gritted his teeth.

"Are you there yet?" Chrys sounded too excited.

He should have predicted this. "Yes."

"Is it all bloody and gross and shit?" They may have caught a couple of killers, but neither had actually viewed a murder scene. Spencer wondered if she was sitting there with popcorn.

He pointed the smartphone screen down at the floor as he backed into the hallway. He walked with one hand against the wall. "I haven't found the room yet."

"Are you breathing heavy?" There was a crunch over the phone line. Spencer was pretty sure it was popcorn being chewed. "Are you afraid?"

With every step the floor creaked. "What do you think? I don't know what I'm doing, I don't know what I'm looking for and you're calling me in the middle of it."

"I'm just trying to help."

"How is this helping, Chrys? You're making me more paranoid than I already am. I'm in an abandoned trailer looking for a murder scene. I don't know if security is coming around or anything."

"Here, hold on a minute. I'm sending you something." A few moments later the phone beeped. "Check it out."

Spencer looked at his screen. Instantly the shadows seemed to move in on him. His sister had sent him a text. He opened it quickly and saw that it was a collection of pictures. His finger touched it and the picture grew to full screen. It was a picture of a room just like the one he had just left, except for obvious differences. There was blood on the floor and a knife roll laid out on the desk; three knives were out of their slots. A chair lay its side next to the bed. In another photo he saw a wire hanging down from the ceiling. "Chrys, what the hell is this?"

"Pics of the scene after the body was removed. Do you like?"

"How did you get this?"

Crunch, crunch "I called in a favor."

"How did you get this?" Spencer was serious this time.

Chrys sighed. "I called Dawn and told her what you were doing. She thinks you're fucking nuts by the way." Dawn had been Chrys' girlfriend once. She was working at an RCMP post up north.

"I don't care what Dawn thinks of me." As long as she never told Chrys what happened it was all good. He thought they were done with her. "She just sent you these pictures?"

She let out a laugh. "Yeah and it's totally illegal, so don't spread the word."

"Are you two getting together again?"

"No way. I told her I'm interested in someone."

Spencer shook his head. This was his sister. Somehow she got into these things and by some magic got herself out. A bead of sweat ran down the side of his face. He grabbed the next door knob and opened it.

This room was the same as the first except there was no desk. His breath caught. A face looked back at him through the window. His face. There were no curtains either. His distorted reflection stared back at him. He dropped his eyes.

"You okay?" The voice on the phone asked.

Spencer took a breath before moving back to the hallway. "Who's the new guy?"

"What new guy?"

"Your new crush."

"It's the new tattoo artist across the street. The woman."

"Swear off men again?"

"After the last one…yeah."

"The last one wore dresses, so does he really count?"

The third door was open. As he stepped through the threshold, he could see everything inside. The bare desk was against the wall. The bed was situated under the window. The dangling cord from the picture was gone now, but the chair was still on its side and there was a dark stain on the floor. "I'm here."

"Oh, you found it?"

In his mind Spencer saw Chrys slide to the edge of her seat. He took a step into the room and immediately felt like he was doing something wrong. His stomach churned. He had the overwhelming feeling of being watched. Still, he couldn't stop his feet from stepping inside.

An odor remained. It was different from the other rooms in that it was more animalistic, something organic. Tessa had been in here for a few days dead or dying – rotting away. The knives were gone; however, there was a mark in the dust on the desk where the knife roll had been. He didn't see any finger marks there. The edge of the desk had been cleared of dust. Perhaps someone needed to hide finer marks. Of course it could have been Tessa fumbling around. The police would have checked that. The dark area on the floor had a couple of flies stuck to what he assumed was dried blood.   It had soaked into the carpeting, hence leaving the odor. Spencer got to his knees and put the phone down as he took a closer look. The blood had pooled for some time. There was a smear on one side possibly cause by where a leg of the chair. Some of the marks dripped along a line as if Tessa had been swinging while she bled. There were very few drip marks between the desk and the dark spot.

"Hey Chrys, do you remember what Caroline said Tessa's injuries were?"

"Yeah, give me a sec … two small stab wounds to her chest and abdomen – not very deep, four cuts to her wrists and two stab wounds to her throat."

Spencer moved to the desk. He moved his face and the light as close to the desk as he could. Dust moved with his breath. As he stood up he said, "There's no blood on the desk."

"But in the picture the knives were on the desk. She should have been bleeding all over the place. What about the floor?"

"I don't see much. Not between where she was hung and the desk." He slowly moved the light to the floor. "I'm also wondering where she would have gotten the extension cord. These rooms look stripped. People took what they wanted. I doubt there'd be a forgotten extension cord and, even if there was, could she tie it with bloody hands? She wouldn't be able to grip it." Spencer looked up at the ceiling. The trailer had a dropped tile ceiling. He wondered if the tiles were made of asbestos. One was missing and through that he could see solid beams running across the building. Spencer put the chair back on its feet. Climbing onto it and reaching up he could easily touch the beam, but he was six feet tall. Tessa was just over five and a half … would she have had the energy to get the cord around the beam? "How could the police think this was suicide?"

"From what my people told me, there are only a few RCMP officers for a long stretch of highway. They and the closest doctor agreed on the suicide."

"Your people?"

"Yeah. I have people."

"Okay. I'm going to take some pictures of the room and then get out of here. I'll call you tomorrow." Before his sister could protest anything else Spencer hit the red button to hang up.

As soon as he was outside, he sat on one of the built-in deck benches and breathed in the fresh air. The cool breeze felt good against his skin. He could still smell that room. He wondered if it was just in his head or if the smell was stuck to the hairs inside his nostrils. Wind shot between the tunnel made by the two trailers. It rejuvenated his brain. Behind him he heard the leaves of willow bushes flapping. Something fluttered overhead. A bird? A bat? Spencer's body shivered. The wind chilled, but it wasn't enough to make him cold. It was fear and the decrease of his adrenaline that made him shiver. He took one more deep breath and blew it out.

This time he kept the flashlight off. Rocks crunched beneath his shoes. The deer were gone. He put his earbud headphones in and turned the music back on. Ed Sheeran sang in his ears. He tried not to think about what had happened in that small room, but when you tried not to think of something that was all that could you *could* think of. Tessa had been tortured with her own knives. After being stabbed and cut she was strung up by the cord. He imagined her up on her toes trying to keep her balance. Her body would have been getting weaker all the time. He knew a little something about being tortured. He hoped it was quick, but knew the odds. The question he really had to figure out was why. If she was tortured - why? Did they have a reason or were they in need of a good time? Was it a mission killer or a complete nutter? He knew a little about people who killed for fun, if you could really call them people.

Spencer pulled out one earbud. His feet shuffled as he turned. Headlights made him block them with his hand. He was in the light of Northview, so how long had the vehicle been behind him? He stopped walking and let the white SUV pull up beside him.

"Stanley, hey." Spencer felt the knot in his chest settle.

"What was your name again?" His voice was flat.

"Spencer; how's it going?"

"What are you doing out here so late?" The old man's expression was flat. The look of his stern eyes made Spencer feel guilty. Yesterday he was the jovial chauffeur. Today he's a serious security guard.

Spencer glanced behind the SUV in the direction of the mountain. "I couldn't sleep and thought I'd walk around for a bit, burn some energy, figure out how long it takes to get to work."

"What were you doing at the trailers?"

Oh shit. Spencer couldn't lose it now. He had to channel his sister's way of bullshitting herself out of everything. "Chef Sam said people went in there to get things they needed. I was looking for a chair."

"Find one?"

"No, not what I wanted. I didn't go in many rooms though." Spencer nodded a few times. He just wanted to get out of there.

Stanley pursed his lips and stared at him for a long pause. "Hop in and I'll give you a ride down the hill."

"No, I'm good."

"Come on, hop in. There's lots of wildlife out in the dark." He pushed the lever to unlock the doors.

Spencer nodded again. They always told kids not to get into cars with strangers, but really did being an adult make a difference in the equation? Everyone was suspect. Everyone could be dangerous. In five minutes he was in his room at Birch Grove with the deadbolt turned and the chain lock fastened.

It was then Spencer realized the night dew had soaked through his clothes chilling him to his bones. In the bathroom he peeled off his shirt and took a moment to check himself in the mirror. The scars were still there. He had been cut many times, no more than skin deep, but months later they were still there together with the hidden emotions. He had good muscle tone (almost a six-pack), so recovering from the torture was going well. Maybe Tessa was better off that she didn't have to live with that. He locked the bathroom door before stripping off his pants and stepping into the shower.

Chapter 5

"Are you Spencer?" One of the white security SUVs pulled across where he was walking to the clubhouse and stopped.

Before he got to the parking lot Spencer had seen trucks loading the old staff trailers. It had been two days and every time he stepped outside he looked over at them and wondered if he'd missed something. Sherlock Holmes would have found something. But he was a fictional character and there was always a clue waiting to be found. He slipped his backpack from his shoulders and let it hang from two fingers. After two days of walking up and down the hill (keeping up appearances – as he told himself) he still missed waking up, stumbling down the stairs at The Alcrest. He didn't mind the walk and felt his leg muscles straining, but there was something to be said about living right above where you work. "Can I help you with something?"

The guard didn't get out of the truck. He leaned out the driver's window and flicked the end of a cigarette dropping the ash to the pavement. "You Spencer?"

"Yes."

"I read a report that you were in the trailers the other night. Is that right?" His skin was tanned. Bushy eyebrows flexed above reflective power sunglasses. The back of his head was shaved short – high and tight around ears which stuck out a little. The name tag on his shirt read Trent.

"Yeah, I was …"

"What were you doing over there?"

Spencer's eyes flicked to the clubhouse to see Amam looking out the screen door. He looked back at the guard. "I needed a chair."

"Did you find one?"

"No, I got a little spooked and left before looking too much."

Trent gazed out the windshield at the workers pulling the second trailer onto a flatbed. "How many rooms did you look in?" His voice was flat. He was acting like he didn't care. Spencer did the same when his sister was telling a story.

"I don't remember really. One or two. Why? What's going on?"

"Those trailers weren't safe. That's why we're getting rid of them." He took a drag from the cigarette and blew out so the wind took the smoke. "I have to make sure you didn't get hurt or anything. If you need a chair contact human resources."

"Will do."

Trent flicked the cigarette away. "You said you only went in two rooms?"

"Yeah," Spencer glanced at the cigarette butt on the ground before looking back at the guard. This was not where he wanted to be. Why did this guy care about what he had done a few nights ago? Here Spencer was needing a low profile and he was getting scolded for screwing around. This wasn't about safety.

"And you didn't see any chairs?"

"I told you I didn't. I have to get to the kitchen." Without another word Spencer walked away from the truck. He couldn't help wondering what he had done though to make this man talk to him. Maybe he was just interested in keeping everyone safe. What did he do when he went in the trailer? Where did he step? What did he touch? The chair … he turned the chair upright in the room where Tessa was killed. Did he put it back on its side? He must have. No, he didn't. They obviously knew he was in the room, so why not just say it?

"You're late." Kitchens were noisy entities. Ovens have motors that run constantly, the exhaust fan is forever moaning, knives are chopping, the dishwasher gets closed with a slam and bursts to life and the radio is always on. Amam's voice was well above the point of being heard.

Spencer stopped with one foot in the staff bathroom. "I was talking to …"

Amam slammed his knife onto the table beside a cutting board. "I don't care. Late is late." His Arabic accent was thick. Dark eyes stared across the kitchen.

It was your typical restaurant kitchen. Stainless steel everything. White tile. Every flat surface was used to hold something. Left over buckets and pails became utensil and product holders. This kitchen had laminated photographs of what each dish was supposed to look like taped to one wall. There was no opening to the dining room. All they had was a tiny glass window on the swinging door and even that was blocked by the service station. Steel, heat, sharp knives, challenging personalities … it was surprising more killings didn't happen in the back of restaurants.

Spencer stepped into the bathroom, closed the door and stared at himself in the mirror. Even his eyes looked tired. He forced himself to take deep breaths. For two days he sat back and let the Egyptian growl and bark orders to do this and that as if Spence was nothing more than a prep-cook bitch. He knew he was supposed to be the boss, but since he didn't plan on being there long he didn't want to rock the boat. He'd put his time in being yelled at by overbearing chefs. At some point enough would be enough.

The kitchen had a completely different feel than The Alcrest, where it was open concept. While back home the cooks were out in the dining room being watched, here they were in the back hidden away. The servers came back, picked up their plates and left. Cooks didn't get to know what their reaction was and nobody was watching what they were doing and keeping them in check.

Customers ate here only due convenience anyway. Nobody really went out of their way to come eat here; this restaurant was merely overflow for when the lodge was full. The cooks seemed to know it and didn't care as much as Spencer was used to.

As he stepped from the bathroom he saw that Amam had moved his work station to the back room. Spencer had to hurry up and get out there.

~ * ~

"How's the case going?" Chrys asked over the phone. Her voice echoed.

Spencer sat on his bed with his back against the wall. A take-out container was open beside him. At Northview they had a basic breakfast for the early golfers then burgers, fries, club sandwiches and salads at lunch time. For the evening menu they still cooked those common meals, but also did a Chinese food menu. It made absolutely no sense. He had brought home sesame soy Shanghai noodles and a beef stir-fry with his own mixture of sauce instead of the spicy sauce they used for the order. He had wooden chopsticks instead of a fork. "I haven't really done much on it. I want to get my feet wet and meet some people."

"Have you talked to Louise Chambers yet?"

"I haven't seen her yet."

"Have you been looking?"

"Yes, Chrys. We work at different golf courses. You don't know how far apart these places are and I work later than others, so we don't pass each other or anything. Didn't I tell you to stay out of this?"

"If I stay out of this, nothing'll get done."

"Do you have me on speaker phone?"

Chrys blasted a breath in frustration. "Do you even have suspects?"

"Chrys," Spencer chewed and swallowed a piece of broccoli, "I don't even know for sure that a crime happened."

"You don't think …"

"I know it looks like something went on …"

"I've been reading her journals, Spence. This girl loved life. She dealt with some crappy stuff in her life and never got down. Being alone wasn't going to …"

"Chrys, stop it." Spencer put down his chopsticks. He could have hung up on her, but knew she'd call back and wouldn't stop until he answered. "I knew Tessa. You didn't. I know what she was like. I'm telling you I don't know yet what happened. I spoke to Bobbi and Stuart about her a little, but everyone sticks with the people that work in their restaurant for the most part. Tessa worked up in the resort kitchen. I have to get up to the resort somehow. Anyway, what are you doing?"

"Going out," she said quickly before returning to what she wanted to talk about. "How are you going to get into the resort? When are you going to go?"

He went back to eating his food. "I don't know. Why do you keep avoiding my questions?"

"I'm not avoiding anything. I have to go. We're almost at the place."

"Chrys …" The phone went quiet. His sister would have already found a way into the lodge and would have been spewing out theories about what happened. She also liked to party to the point of excess. Leaving her in charge of the restaurant was probably not the right move.

Chapter 6

"Why did you do such a shitty job cleaning the grill?" Amam's words were thick with his Arabic accent and his dark eyes glowered at Spencer. He leaned forward slightly as if he were towering his weight over the other man. His hands were in tight fists making his knuckles white. "Stuart said he had to clean it again when he came this morning."

Spencer looked around the olive-skinned man to the breakfast cook. His eyes were down on the peppers he was dicing. Bobbi was scrubbing pans at the dishpit sink. She looked in their direction with a timid glance before moving her attention back on her job.

Spencer had just arrived, ten minutes early, and didn't even have time to change into the staff uniform of a white chef coat and black pants before Amam started in on him. His shift started at 1:00 pm and lasting until closing. He had been working with Kevin in the evenings, but let the younger cook go early last night as a favor.

It took only ten minutes on his first day to realize Amam was a male chauvinistic pig who thought Bobbi's (and every other woman's) place in a restaurant kitchen was doing the dishes and that was it. He flirted with the female servers, but they didn't step inside his world. He showed up at 11:00 am and started doing what was basically the sous chef's job. From what Spencer was told he'd yell at Bobbi the moment she walked through the door at noon. He got angry at the least provocation and blasted in whoever's direction he wanted to throw it at – usually Bobbi's even if it wasn't her fault. Spencer had worked for chefs and owners of restaurants that were as mean as they could be and Amam was just another one of those.

Kevin came out of the staff bathroom. He showed up on time and was dressed in chef clothes, the sleeves rolled up past his elbows. His head was shaved smooth, but his goatee was long. The moustache hairs curled down over his upper lip. After working with him for two nights, Spencer knew more about this young man's life than he wanted to know. He was twenty-six, supported two kids back in Ontario, however wasn't with their mother and had every woman who worked for the resort listed on the Kevin Scale. He was great at getting information on everyone that worked there and he spoke freely. As soon as Spencer's eyes met his the younger man's dropped to the floor.

"Kevin say you stayed to clean the grill." Amam's voice was a lot louder than it needed to be. "Why would you not clean it?"

"I did clean it." Spencer knew when he left last night that he had not done a fantastic job cleaning the flat-top grill, but it wasn't horrible. He hadn't worked with one of those in a few years.

"Stuart has pictures. You did not clean it." Spit flew from his Amam's lips.

Spencer took a step back. He actually felt his shoulders start to slump. It had been a long time since anyone bullied him and he really didn't like it.

Amam grabbed a tomato and tossed it hard toward the garbage can. It exploded in a red mess of flesh, juice and seed against the wall behind it. "Why didn't you clean it?"

Low profile. Spencer had to remember low profile. He could take someone bitching at him. He looked at the other crew standing around. A server had just walked through the door from the dining room. She put the dirty plates down in the dishpit and got the hell out.

Amam's hand came down on a cutting board. The plastic board jumped. His fingers touched the handle of a French knife and made it move.

Fuck it. "WHO THE HELL DO YOU THINK YOU ARE?" Spencer couldn't control himself. His eyes burned. He felt the veins popping out in his neck. "I'm YOUR boss remember? I'm the one going to the chef meeting today – not you. You're not the chef. If I do a piss poor job you talk to me about it. You sure as hell don't throw things."

"I will throw what I want. You just got here. You have no say over what I do." It was Amam's turn to take a step back, but he tried sticking out his chest like a bird trying to make a statement.

"Do you want me to call Chef and see what he thinks? You throw one more thing and I will. I'll make sure your ass is out of MY kitchen. In here you're my bitch." This was what he called keeping a low profile? Back home he had to raise his voice a few times, usually at Chrys, but he always tried to remain calm. The power that surged through him now was invigorating. He realized his hands were in fists, the fingernails biting into his palms. His body shook. He was ready if the bigger man made a move toward him or if his long fingers closed around the handle of the knife. He waited a moment with the two of them staring at each other before saying, "Why don't you go organize the dry storage."

Amam stared at him. His lips were so tight the Egyptian's skin was pulled across his face. Spencer looked down and saw his fingers curl. At least he was away from the knife. Without a sound the chef d'partie walked off in the direction of the back storage room.

Spencer disappeared into the staff washroom and closed the door. The work schedule was on the wall next to a Hand Washing poster. Amam worked 11:00 am to 7:00 pm and did not have a day off for two days. That meant for six hours every day the two of them had to occupy the same space. Spencer himself wasn't supposed to have a day off until Saturday. It was now Tuesday. They had already spent three days together and now they were stuck together with all this tension for a couple more days. At least it was two days in a row. Plus somehow he had to investigate what happened to Tessa. He was getting that *stuck* feeling like there was nowhere to run.

As soon as Spencer stepped out dressed in his chef coat and black pants Kevin asked, "Do you mind if I leave early? Stewart's here and we're not busy and all that, man. I got tomorrow off, so I want to start getting ready for tonight. I want to go sit in the hot springs and soak a while. I'm off in forty minutes anyway."

"Yeah, go ahead."

"You coming to karaoke tonight?" Kevin asked but just got a shake of the head in return. "Half the resort staff goes. It's a good time, bro." He took his chef coat off and hung it on a hook.

"I don't know." It really wasn't Spencer's thing, however he could use it to meet people. He could see how everyone reacted around each other. "We'll see how I feel after work."

~ * ~

"How are things going?" Chef Sam asked as Spencer climbed into the passenger side of the truck two hours later.

Spencer wasn't sure how much he wanted to tell the man. "There have been some personality conflicts. I guess that's the best way to put it."

"Amam? Is it him and Bobbie again?"

"No. Me and him. We both have different ideas on what his job is and what my job is."

"You're the boss. He has to fall in line. His brother is the sous chef at The Valley, you'll meet him in the meeting. I've had trouble with Amam before. He's a good cook, but he needs to learn to do things the Canadian way." Sam slowed the truck to move around some riders coming out of the horse pen. "For starters he thinks women shouldn't be in a professional kitchen. Have you put Bobbie on the line?"

Spencer checked his phone. There were no messages from his sister today. "A bit, always after Amam leaves for the day. She's too nervous to go online otherwise."

Sam smiled and his gums showed. "No matter how many times I tell him to let her cook he won't do it. Everyone in the kitchen should be able to cook. I'm sorry to put you in this position, but it's your job now to straighten it out. I've been stretched so thin I can't seem to do anything."

Spencer was tempted to tell Chef that he wasn't planning on sticking around for too long. He'd do what he could while he was there out of love for the profession and those who want to do it. However, when his real job here was done he was gone. He had a restaurant back home to run. He followed the chef after the truck was parked outside the main lodge. Three men stood away from the door smoking cigarettes. Two of them wore chef coats.

"Spencer, sous chef at Northview - this is Karl, sous chef for Spring Lounge here in the main building, Rehu, sous chef at The Valley and Gregory, our sommelier for the entire resort."

Rehu was a big man with a firm body. His arms and legs were thick with muscle. His skin was dark, like Amam, and they both had the same intense gaze. He put his fingers on his cigarette and made no motion toward the new cook except to stare at him.

Karl stepped forward with his hand out. This cook was tall and thin with the start of a beard on his cheeks and his hair greased back. When he smiled there was an obviously broken tooth in the front. His hand shake was not as firm as the sommelier, however.

For a man who chose the perfect wine to go with a meal his grip was awfully firm. He wore a crisp expensive-looking shirt and his hair was perfectly groomed. He looked at the new man with deep blue eyes. Spencer felt uncomfortable with all of them.

Rehu dropped his hand-rolled cigarette to the paved parking lot and gently turned a pointed shoe to crush the butt without ever lifting the heel. "You work with my brother," he said with a thick accent.

At first Spencer didn't realize he was being spoken to then noticed everyone was quiet and looking in his direction. He gave a slight nod and didn't say a word. The dark-skinned man crossed his arms over his thick chest. "He says you don't know what you're doing."

Spencer stared at him. He had gone to school to become a chef. He had worked his ass off. He owned a semi-successful restaurant. The last thing he needed was the brother of a chauvinistic power hungry prick saying crap about him or his talent. Screw blending in. "Well your brother is an ass-hat, so I would take anything he says with a grain of salt." He watched the man's lips purse together so tight it must have hurt. Spencer curled his fingers into fists to be ready for what was coming.

"Gentlemen," Chef Sam took a step so that he was almost between them, "we should be getting inside." He kept his gaze on the bigger man.

Rehu stared at him a long moment before being the first to walk inside.

Karl slapped Spencer's shoulder as he walked pass and declared, "I like you."

Spencer waited until the others went into the lodge before he followed. The happy twins were at the front desk. A woman flashed him a smile as she walked toward the spa. The parking lot was full, so every room was probably booked. Gazing up the steps, he saw a dozen or so people in the lounge. That was more than they had at Northview all day. The room was more elegant than his new temporary restaurant. The dining room down at the golf course was decorated in mountain-golf chic with a mountain goat head and old clubs on the walls. This one was more about the beauty of the mountain horizon. Large windows provided a panorama view of the hot spring pools and the western mountain range across the valley. The sunsets from here were probably amazing.

"Hey boss, you coming to the pool?" Kevin stood beside Spencer with three glasses of golden liquid held in his long fingers.

Spencer shook his head. "Chef meeting."

"Too bad. I'm working on two hot babes from Middleton. I can't decide whether to go blond or brunette." Kevin's elbow tapped his boss's arm as he nodded toward the window.

Standing beside the pool was a slender woman with soft, almost caramel skin. Spencer let his eyes travel over lithe firm legs. The bikini bottoms had a black and grey zigzag pattern that reminded him of the pattern on Charlie Brown's T-shirt. She didn't care who saw her pick a wedge. He thought it looked familiar. So did the tiny birthmark on her lower back. Her hair, he assumed to be chestnut, was almost black from being wet. The woman made a conscious effort to cover her right ear with it. Spencer knew who she was, but this woman had a colourful flower tattoo on the back of her left shoulder. The woman he knew shouldn't have a tattoo. She better not have one.

"That's the brunette," Kevin stated. "Hot tattoo right? She says it's a chrysanthemum."

"She does, does she?" Spencer watched the woman turn around. She paused a moment until she saw the two men and started walking toward them. He stared at her deep brown eyes, because he really didn't need to be looking at the bikini-clad body of his sister.

She made sure that each step had purpose and though everyone was looking at her she really didn't notice or didn't care. Chrys had that way about her. She knew she was good-looking and sexy, but didn't let on that she knew. Spencer knew he should find the other chefs, but he couldn't move. He wanted to find out what the hell she was doing here, but he couldn't say anything in front of the others.

She didn't stop walking as she reached the two men. Her finger grazed Spencer's chef coat and she said, "You dripped."

Spencer looked down at the spot where he had dribbled some sauce he had tasted earlier. He spun in the direction she walked. "Are you going to karaoke?"

Chrys raised a hand in the air, the middle finger raised high. She turned a corner and was gone.

"You have a way with the ladies," Kevin slapped his shoulder.

Spencer grunted. "She's no lady."

Chapter 7

Spencer heard the beat of music long before he got to the front door of the bar. The parking lot was almost full. After he finished work he washed the sweat off as best he could in the staff bathroom, slicked his hair back reviving the blond spikes and walked to the village. Had he known he was going there this morning he would have brought a change of clothes. As it was he was in black kitchen pants and the T-shirt he wore under his chef coat. His sister still hadn't answered any of the texts he had sent, so he hoped she got the hint to meet him at the bar. That is if she bothered to find out where karaoke was taking place.

As he opened the door, loud conversation and music almost pushed him back into the night. His senses were overwhelmed. He smelled sweat, perfume and liquor all mingling together. It was dark inside with spotlights near the stage. As his eyes became accustomed to the dimness, he recognized both employees and guests of the resort.

Kevin was sitting at the bar talking to a tall slender woman wearing denim shorts and a white muscle shirt that fit snugly around her body. She rubbed her nose and Spencer knew who it was. How his sister convinced the woman (the two honestly hated each other) to come here was the real question. His eyes searched the crowd of people looking for any sign of his sister. If Hanni was up here Chrys had to be somewhere.

"Who's your friend?" Spencer yelled into Kevin's ear to be heard over the loud music. A man with a round belly was on stage doing his best rendition of Ring of Fire.

Kevin's eyes were droopy. "This is Honey. She's the one I told you about. I don't know where her friend is." He twisted so fast to locate her that he almost fell from the stool.

Spencer put his hand out to the woman who had worked for him the past couple of years as a server. "Nice to meet you, Hanni."

She raised an eyebrow as she sipped her drink. Her long blond hair was loose. She was the dictionary definition of being "all legs." The shorts were so short and top so tight she left very little to the imagination. Her greatest talent at The Alcrest was flirting her way into giant gratuities - that and making Spencer nervous.

He felt a hand on his back. His body tensed and he held his breath. There was someone close to him, pressed up against him. "I booked a song for us to sing together."

Spencer exhaled and sucked in perfumed oxygen. He stared into the dark eyes of his foster-sister. "I'm Spencer."

"Chrys." Full lips formed into a smile with bright teeth behind which the strange bar lighting made to almost glow. "We're going to sing *Need You Now* by Lady Antebellum."

"Isn't that a love song? We just met." Spencer felt someone bump against him. His stomach churned with the closeness of everyone.

"It's just a song." She picked up a beer and took a quick drink. She leaned in close to her brother's ear on the side opposite where Kevin stood and said, "We should talk."

"Where? We just met, remember."

"Let's go outside for a smoke."

"Neither of us smoke." Spencer felt that was an important point. He added, "Unless that's something else you've kept hidden."

Chrys gave him the most sinister smirk she could manage. Her brother could be fun at times (well she had heard stories) but he could also be a real stick in the mud. He liked getting paperwork done before going out – on those rare occasions that he went out. She wore tight black jeans and a plaid shirt with enough buttons open to see the top line of a sapphire bra. It was sexy, but far more conservative than Hanni's top. A lot more of her was covered than in the afternoon. "You better have a drink. I bet you're too chicken-shit to sing with me." Chrys pulled Hanni toward her and said something so close her lips touched the other woman's ear.

Spencer had gone out with the work crew singing before and it did take a healthy amount of alcohol to get him behind the mic. Chrys could do it straight up. Hell, she didn't need a reason or event to start singing.

Hanni took Kevin by the hand and led him toward the door.

As soon as they were gone, Chrys pulled her brother in close and said, "I thought you'd need some help," right into his ear.

Spencer felt her hot breath. He put his lips next to her ear. "I'm doing fine."

"Really? What suspects do you have?"

Spencer didn't say anything. He barely knew anyone who worked at the resort except for his own crew. He didn't have one suspect. He wasn't even convinced Tessa was murdered.

"That's what I thought. I have suspects from Tessa's letters and emails. I've met half the lodge staff in one day and I've done some asking around. Face it, Spence, no matter how cute and good you are at your job, a hot chick can find out a lot more info in a short amount of time. It's our turn to sing."

After two rapid shots of tequila, not very good tequila, Spencer followed Chrys to the stage. If singing a romantic song with his little sister wasn't awkward enough, halfway through she grabbed his hand. It made it uncomfortable enough that it actually seemed like this could have been the first time they met. Near the end of the song Spencer had located almost all of his staff in the crowd watching him, everyone except Amam. As soon as he was off the stage, he got another tequila.

"That was really good." Hanni stared at Spencer. Her eyes looked glassy. She and Kevin had found a table.

"I told you, you could do it. I need some air." Chrys had to yell at her brother as a group of servers from The Valley were well into their rendition of *Love Shack* by the B52's.

Spencer hadn't been working there long enough, nor mingled with other resort staff, to truly recognize anyone. He saw Kent, the Spring Lounge sous chef, at a table, but didn't know anyone else in the crowd. When he and Chrys were singing, he saw Blaire from the front desk in a very close embrace with the man she had been working with. He wondered if they had a relationship before working together or if the mountains created the perfect romantic setting. Most of Northview's servers were at one table. He looked around slowly to see if he recognized anyone else.

Spencer squinted to see who had just walked in. It was a stroke of luck he didn't come in a few minutes earlier when they were up on stage. Spencer snatched Chrys' arm and pulled her close to him. He held her tight to stop her from struggling and pressed his lips against her ear. "Remember Jonas, the crazy guy I fired two months ago? He just walked in."

Chrys looked at the door. When she turned back to Spencer her eyes had gone wide. Jonas had only worked a couple of shifts at The Alcrest Gastropub before being fired for being a moron who couldn't follow orders. He returned to the restaurant and threw a can of paint through the plate glass window. If he recognized either of them, this whole thing could be shot. "Want to join me?" Chrys yelled at her brother.

He nodded as soon as he saw his former cook head toward the bathrooms.

Chrys got the car keys from Hanni and whispered what they had seen into her ear as they left.

As Spencer walked away, he felt fingernails scape over his butt cheek and flinched. It was Hanni's thing. If he told her he was used to it and didn't care anymore, she would probably stop doing it. He didn't want to do that. Her favorite time to grab his ass was in front of his girlfriend, which never went over well.

"What the hell is Jonas doing here?" Spencer held his sister's arm as she directed the way to the car.

"I've been at the lodge all day and I didn't see him."

"Maybe he works at The Valley. I hope he works at The Valley." He squeezed her arm. "Who have you been talking to?"

Chrys twisted her arm from his grip. "A few people. I've been telling everyone I'm a reporter and I have suspects."

"Who?"

She bit her tongue until they were inside the car at the far end of the lot. "Tessa wrote to Caroline about some guy named Karl. She thought he was creepy and scary."

"He seems nice enough to me. What are you doing here, Chrys? Why would you bring Hanni?"

"We're a team, Spence. You and me, not me and Hanni. She's just the slut I needed to give me a ride. I can't leave you up here alone with killers."

"Since when is it killers, plural?"

"Tessa wrote in an email that she thought a few guys were watching her. She never mentioned names exactly, but there always seemed to be the same guys around. I printed out every text she sent and I have copies of her hand-written letters. I know, who does that, right?" She turned around in the passenger seat and tried reaching a cardboard tomato box she'd taken from their restaurant. Her finger tips touched the lid, but couldn't quite get it.

"Chrys, forget it. I can't look at them right now anyway. You shouldn't be here. Who's watching The Alcrest?"

She left the box where it was. They both looked toward the bar. A few people stood outside the doors giving themselves lung cancer. "Jess is. Gordie wanted help in the kitchen, so I called Patrick Healy. He's a crazy old guy."

"He was there when Dad ran it and Dad fired him. Do you know what will happen with him and Gordie together? We won't have a restaurant to go home to. He loves practical jokes. He used to throw cherry bombs into the dishpit to terrify the dishwasher."

"So?"

"I was the dishwasher."

"You always said he was an amazing cook and taught you a lot."

"He was, but the old goat needs supervision." Spencer had enjoyed learning from Patrick through all the years he had been with The Alcrest back when it was a pub. He was the one who got Spencer to lower his hands (palm down and fingers spread apart) onto the hot flat-top over and over as long as he could stand it to build the toughness in his hands and fingers. It sounds cruel; however, for a chef it was invaluable. "Anyway, it's too late now. Why did you have to bring Hanni?"

"Afraid you can't keep your hands off her?" Her face turned to an ugly sneer. "I needed a ride. She's just going to lay around the pool all day the whole time trying to pick up rich business men and maybe get a tan on her pasty-white legs."

Spencer breathed before getting into the argument again. "Chrys, you two have to leave. I can handle things here."

Her face wrinkled. "Fuck you. I've already paid for three days, so I'm staying here. When do you work?"

"Tomorrow from 1:00 pm to close. I have Thursday off."

"Then I'll work on getting to know the staff at the lodge while you do whatever it is you do." She saw a couple exit the bar.

Spencer leaned back against the passenger seat. He could yell and argue – she'd agree to leave – but she'd do what she wanted anyway. "So what the hell is that thing I saw on your shoulder?" There was no point fighting her on anything else.

"My ink," she said with sarcastic pride.

"Is it permanent?"

"What do you think?"

"What's Mom going to say?"

Chrys saw the dark shadow people coming in their direction. "That it's my body and I can do what I want with it."

"Oh you think so?"

"Well that is what she said when I told her before I even did it. She also helped me pick the flower, so there. Someone's coming."

"What if it's Jonas? He can't see us." He may not recognize Chrys, but he would definitely know Spencer.

"They're getting closer." Chrys grabbed Spencer's arm digging her nails into his flesh. Her brother couldn't see without turning. They were only a couple of car lengths away. The girls had parked the car in the far corner of the lot because the lighting was poor and Chrys knew she'd have to talk to her brother somewhere. This was bad. They had to hide. Jumping in the back seat was ridiculous. They had to hide their faces.

Chrys grabbed he brother by the shirt. She pulled him into her as she moved forward and pushed her lips against his. Spencer tried to move back and Chrys quickly pushed her hand against the back of his head. As long as tongues didn't move she was good. She had acted in plays. She could hold this. They weren't blood related, so it was just a little creepy.

The knock on the door window made her jump. Her heart was in her throat.

Spencer pushed away. The back of his head cracked against the passenger window.

The driver's door opened turning on the overhead light. Hanni's face was there. Her red lips formed into the Joker's smile - one of the wicked ones when he was doing extreme evil and Batman was nowhere to be found.

"You kids ready to go?" Hanni held the tip of her tongue between her teeth as her smile grew and her eyes went from one to the other. Kevin was behind her oblivious to what was going on inside the automobile.

Chrys kept her gaze down. She pushed at her brother motioning for him to get out of the car so that she could slide over the middle console into the passenger seat. She ran the back of her hand across her lips.

His fingers gripped the back of his head. His sister shows up and in just a few hours he was injured. Typical.

Chapter 8

"Why are you up so early, bitch?"

"I have to meet my brother." Chrys had showered, dried and dressed and was now brushing her long hair in front of the mirror in their hotel room.

Hanni looked up at her. "Can't you do that in the bathroom?"

"I fogged up the mirror."

"Why do you have to meet your *lover* so early anyway?"

"He has to work. And I said brother."

"You were the one sucking face with him last night. I thought maybe your relationship had changed." Hanni twisted her body and pulled the blankets over her head.

Chrys slammed her brush onto the dresser. "We weren't sucking face. I had to make what's-his-face think something was going on. And I didn't know it was you. It could have been that Jonas guy." When they'd returned back to the hotel room she had gone over the highlights. Hanni didn't really care at the time. She just stripped and got into bed.

"Yeah right. You've probably been wanting to kiss him forever. I should have taken a picture and sent it to Jessie."

At that Chrys almost fell over. She was struggling to get her Steve Madden ankle boots on, so she was certain that was the reason. The heels were enough to make her legs flex and her ass tighten. "First off, eww he's my brother. And second, she'd go fucking nuts."

"I know she would and you're not blood related. And he is a good kisser, so I don't blame you. Turn the light off."

Chrys didn't say anything else. She took Hanni's car keys from where they had been dropped last night, a room key-card and left. She did not turn off the light. Yes, there had been a time back during puberty when Chrys looked at Spencer in a special non-sibling sort of way. Having her friend dare her to take a picture of his Johnson didn't help any. That was a long time ago though and the sibling emotions were too strong. Plus the kiss was so flat and gross she may not want to kiss another human being again. Except for Sloane. She really wanted to kiss her.

Wait, how did Hanni know Spence was a good kisser? For a moment she thought about going back and asking her. She'd ask him instead. Wait, she kissed the same lips as Hanni? "Fuck off."

It was almost 10:00 am, so the main lodge was alive and busy. Both the restaurant and lounge were full of customers. She saw a group heading toward the pools. As her eyes followed them she saw people, mostly men, sitting inside the windows watching the people at the pools. The hot springs were fantastic, but not fantastic enough to be a spectator sport. Perhaps that was the creepy vibe Tessa had.

She stepped to the side to let three men carrying golf bags go by. One mumbled, "We're late. We're late." If he checked a pocket watch Chrys was going to piss herself.

A woman in a terrycloth robe turned away from the front desk and walked the hallway toward the spa. Hanni had reservations for a deep tissue message this afternoon. Chrys had made the mistake of saying she'd go halfers in order to get Hanni to drive here. She was hoping to get in some hand and foot pampering while there herself.

Outside was a small work crew putting up a white log fence on the cliff side of the parking lot. As she reached the car, Chrys caught one of the guys looking at her and gave him a tiny wave and a smile. A cute girl could get a lot of information. A cute smiling flirtatious girl was unstoppable. And those with the most information were usually at the bottom of the latter, so a cute smiling flirtatious girl could find out all she needed to know.

Once she was in the car, she checked the directions Spencer had texted her. He didn't want to meet at the staff quarters or anywhere visible from there. Jonas was somewhere. He might not care about why they were there, but he would surely ask questions and may not be a fan of either of them since the police got involved the last time. She had to go down the hill and turn left before reaching the highway. She'd drive past Northview and stop at the far corner across the street from a brown house with a bridge to the garage. She had no idea what that meant.

She parked across the road from the brown house, and waited ten minutes before she stepped outside. She didn't know how cops could handle stakeouts. She hated waiting. She needed to be constantly moving. That was why she worked at the restaurant, taught dancing, played roller-derby, worked at the locksmiths, went to the gym and took almost every part-time job that came along. Five more minutes and she had gone through her text messages. This spot had good phone service. A dance student's mom wanted to hire her for extra tutoring, the derby team agreed to bump up practices, Sloane wanted to know how the tattoo was and Sue at The Alcrest told her what Gordie and Patrick did last night. She told the mom she would be in touch when she got back, didn't answer about the derby practices and laughed at the restaurant high jinx. The only response she took time writing was to Sloane. There still wasn't anything between the two, but she did ask about the tattoo so that could mean something.

Chrys stretched out on the hood of the car, leaned against the windshield and shut her eyes. The sun came through the trees to warm her face.

"What are you doing?"

Chrys knew that voice. She opened her eyes and looked at the angry, sweaty face of her brother. "What took you so long?"

"Every time I tried getting out of my room I heard voices. I didn't want to be face to face with Jonas, so I waited until they were gone. You're not supposed to be out in the open like this." He checked over his shoulder. The owner of the brown house crossed to the garage.

"Oh yeah because I'm so out in the open." She still hadn't moved. Her legs were crossed at the ankles, she wiggled her feet without realizing. Her dark yoga pants already had dust marks on them.

"Let's go." Spencer squinted behind dark sunglasses. He didn't drink too often, so last night was playing havoc with his head.

"You're such a pain." Chrys slipped to the ground and wiped dirt from her thighs.

The door on the brown garage slowly opened. Spencer glanced at the driver of a charcoal Lincoln SUV as it pulled out and retreated down the hill. It was the same man who had crossed from the house. All he saw was wavy dark hair and dark glasses. He was no Matthew McConaughey.

Spencer directed his sister up the hill into a residential area. They could still be seen by locals; however, nobody who worked at the resort would see them. That was his thought process anyway.

He got her to park on the side of the road. "Where are those letters?"

"In the back seat in the box."

Spencer turned and grabbed the box, the lid was half off already, and brought it forward onto his lap. "Did you just leave this in the car over night?"

"Come on, Spence, nobody has any reason to go through Hanni's car." Chrys watched him fumble through the pages. In the box she had printouts of every email Tessa had sent to her parents and best friend since getting the job at Fontana, printouts of texts, photocopies of hand written letters and some of the journals Chrys had borrowed. "Do you want me to just give you the gist? She got here near the end of winter. From what I read everything was fine for a while. She loved the skiing, liked the people, yada yada. Then after the snow melted she started hiking in the woods."

"Yeah, there are loads of trails all over." Spencer had talked to Bobbi about the area a lot. His time there hadn't been a complete waste.

"Whatever. She then hiked two trails on her next days off in late May and her emails changed. She started getting lonely and stopped doing anything on her days off. She also started having the feeling she was being watched. She didn't go into detail about anything that happened, but it was around that time. Two months later she was dead."

"You think she got killed over a hike?"

"No, Spencer. Maybe she saw something or someone. Maybe it has nothing to do with any of that and it's just a coincidence. I'm trying to help. If you want to be a dick I can go home."

"Good. Go."

"Fuck you." Chrys looked out her window and listened to her brother flip through pages for a while before continuing. "I'm going to keep talking to staff members and see what they know."

"You're going to tip off the killer."

"I'm being careful. Tomorrow we should go for a hike above the resort. Tessa went on two hiking trails that that started there."

"What if you're wrong and we waste our time?" Spencer stacked the papers together.

Chrys said, "Then I'm wrong. We don't have anywhere else to start."

"Fine, but no sticking our necks out." He got the box of papers back into the rear seat. "We're all alone out here."

People were moving around the houses. Through the trees they saw a golf cart drive down a fairway. This was a beautiful place, full of colour and life. It was hard to think a killer could be here too.

"Hanni says you're a good kisser. When did you two kiss?" Chrys didn't care who her brother kissed as long as it wasn't Hanni. The woman was like a wolverine with manicured claws. Hanni didn't care about who got hurt along the way, as long as she got what she needed.

"What are you talking about?" Spencer knew exactly what she was talking about. He didn't want to talk about it at all and was going to have to talk to Hanni about keeping her mouth shut. "What about you kissing me? What was that about?"

Chrys growled as she started the car. "That was about saving your ass. I didn't know who was coming. And while we're talking about it, when was the last time you brushed your teeth? Your breath tasted like funky mushrooms or some shit."

"Oh shut up. I worked all day. I didn't expect my sister to kiss me." To him the kiss was nothing. It was like kissing an old aunt. That was what he told himself, and that was what he was going to believe.

Chrys pulled the car to the side of the road across from the brown house again. The Lincoln was parked in the driveway. A couple of cars went by heading toward Northview. Every time one passed, Spencer flinched, expecting to see a co-worker.

"I'll text you when I'm done work. Try not to get into any trouble."

"You know me."

"That's why I said it." Spencer got out of the car and started walking toward the golf course. He didn't want Chrys in harm's way and wanted to do this himself, however with her here he was already further along than he was the day before.

He heard a car engine behind him and took a quick glance over his shoulder. A white security SUV slowed at the exact spot where he had been dropped off. For a moment he thought it was going to turn and follow him, but the driver gunned the engine and sped past him toward the clubhouse. He recognized the sunglasses of the head of security. Was this part of his job or was he doing a drive-by on Spencer? Why would he do that? Spencer tried to think about what he had done and said. The only thing he could think of was the old staff trailers. Unless Jonas saw and recognized him. He didn't have a choice but to go on. He was getting a bad feeling.

Chapter 9

Hanni was probably still asleep. She put more than alcohol into her system last night, so she was going to be out until her spa appointment. As Chrys exited from the car, she glanced at the Indian bathhouse up on the rocks. In an email Tessa sent to Caroline she included pictures of that; it was from her last hike. What did she stumble upon? Chrys had the urge to head up there herself right now and see what she could find. Her brother would kill her. Not that that ever stopped her before.

A map of hiking trails, alongside notices to watch for bears and cougars, was posted just inside the front doors. Each trail was a different colour. The one going past the bathhouse was blue. As it reached where the bush line would be, it broke into green and red going in different directions. Further on was a yellow trail. Which one did Tessa use? They zig-zagged up and around the mountain before returning.

None crossed the road that led to the ski lodge. Another trail was marked in orange. It started across the RV Park behind the main building and advanced upward on a protruding mountain. *Were they still called mountains if they didn't go that high? The ones behind the lodge were high enough to have snow on their caps.* Chrys knew that Tessa had gone on that trail. She'd taken pictures of signs posted along the way, depicting local plants and wildlife, and attached them to her letter. Perhaps that was where she got into trouble. Her letter for that one was complete though. The one for the other trail didn't seem that way; it felt unfinished. She'd written that she found a deer antler and thought she was lost. The next part of it was a picture of her laying exhausted on her bed. To Chrys there were parts missing.

"Planning a hike?" Blaire's smile was so large that Chrys wondered if it could snap her face. She wore the front desk uniform, the name tag nearly shone and her hair fell nicely with the maroon streak riding the wave over hear ear.

"I'm just looking. Can I get a copy of the hiking trails?"

"Of course." Blaire spun on her heel and bounced to the front desk. Though the other front desk clerk was dealing with someone else, he still found time to flash Blaire a smile. "Here you go. I would consider taking this hill side trail, the orange one. It gives you excellent views of the valley. Plus you can get educated on the flora and fauna of the area as you go. Or if you want a hike that is like going to another planet I would suggest going down the highway to the Hoodoos. It's a natural rock formation..."

"What about these trails?" Chrys pointed to the blue trial and the others that branched off.

"They are good if you like trees and rocks." She flashed a smile that said she didn't. "There isn't much to see up there. The views are all blocked by forest."

"What about the ski hill? Can you hike up there?"

"That's closed and restricted this time of year." Blaire's smile was gone. It returned again in an instant as if a switch was thrown. If Chrys wasn't looking she would have missed the change.

"Can I ask you a question," she made a show of checking out the woman's name tag, "Blaire."

"Of course. We are always here to answer your questions." Smile.

"I want to know about Tessa Knelman." Chrys stared at Blaire. The smile instantly disappeared. The two clerks looked at each other for a moment. "She worked here, right?"

Blaire stuttered a moment. "I didn't know her personally. It was a tragedy."

"So what do you think happened?" A customer stepped up to the counter forcing Chrys to step aside.

"I'm sorry, you'll have to speak to the manager. What was your name again?" Blaire's smile was back, but it didn't reach her eyes. Those burned over the counter.

"You know what? I'll find the manager later. Thanks for your help."

Chrys folded the map and slipped it into her pocket as she walked down the corridor toward the lounge. She felt eyes on her back. She had skipped breakfast, so an early lunch was due. Plus you never know who you can find to talk to.

When Chrys had read Tessa's emails and letters she made sure to take note of any names mentioned. She walked around the dining room focusing on name tags. The staff all seemed to be in their mid-twenties. The moment she saw a server whose name she recognized, she sat in her section. Her name was Hayden and she seemed good at her job. Chrys should know since she wasn't particularly good at the same job back home. The server asked how her day was going and if she had tried the hot spring pools yet. Chrys tried thinking of a way to bring up the dead woman that was a little more subtle than with the front desk folks.

She ate a grilled chicken sandwich with lettuce, tomato and a chipotle mayo, plus bacon, and fries smothered in gravy. Her brother would have grumbled something about chipotle being done to death. All she drank was ice water with a slice of lime. She stared out the window at the pools and the view beyond and went over all of considered the ways to bringing up Tessa in her head. None seemed right.

"How was everything?" Hayden was one of those girls who looked pretty and smart all at the same time. The server uniform here was black slacks and a black golf-shirt. She wrote hers with none of the buttons fastened and a gold chain with an ornate cross dangling over her cleavage.

"Good." If Chrys was going to be honest they could have learned a lot from the food at The Alcrest. This chicken was dry as a rock and the mayo too spicy. "I noticed a lot of the staff are young. Do you like working here?"

Her smile beamed as she gave the cookie-cutter answer. "Certainly."

"Do you know if there are any openings?" Chrys really didn't care, but she was getting ready for what she really wanted to ask.

"Probably. You can check on our website for sure."

Chrys took a quick look around making sure no one was listening. "I heard a girl who worked here committed suicide or something. What about that? The family made a big stink about it in Middleton."

Perspiration formed on Hayden's temples. Her eyes rose and searched the room, her fingers flinched at her side.

"I know it was ruled a suicide," Chrys couldn't help herself, "but there was a lot of talk about …"

The server suddenly knelt over and rested the fingertips of one hand on the table. She glanced over her shoulder. "I can't say anything."

"Why can't you? Did you know her?" Chrys had that tingle in the pit of her stomach. Her pulse raced.

"Yes I did. She was nice."

"She thought something strange was going on. Do you know about anything?"

Hayden's lips pressed together tightly.

"Is there anyone I can talk to about her?" Chrys' eyes scanned the restaurant. No other servers were close by. She hoped she wasn't making a mistake here. "I'm just curious."

Hayden stood up tall. She said, "I'll be right back with your bill," and walked away.

Chrys returned to staring out the window, still holding onto her glass. Her thumb smeared the condensation around the outside. Had she just made a huge mistake? Everyone she talked to could have been the murderer or knew what was going on. Her brother was going to kill her.

"Here you go." Hayden placed a black billfold on the table beside the plate of smeared gravy and leftover burger bun. "Is there anything else that I can get you?"

Chrys flipped open the billfold with one finger. Her bill was there with a handwritten note on the bottom.

"I'll meet you at the register when you're ready."

Chrys' eyes followed the woman as she crossed the room. Hayden walked right past a man in a white chef coat. Chrys' gaze flipped to him and saw that he was staring at her. He smiled (one tooth looked broken) and crossed toward her.

"Hi, I'm Karl one of the kitchen managers." He had whiskers across his face. His hair was slicked back. "I was told you wanted to talk to a manager."

Chrys squeezed her fist around the bill as she got to her feet. She flashed a brilliant smile. "Actually, I'm good. Thank you for your concern though." As she met Hayden at the till and paid for her sandwich, out of the corner of her eye, she saw Karl walk back to the kitchen. He looked in her direction a few times. Was that creepy Karl that Tessa wrote about? She didn't get that feeling about him.

~ * ~

"You're back," Hanni said as she entered the hotel room from the bathroom. She was wrapped in a towel and had another twisted around her head.

"Do you want to go golfing?" Chrys had been in the room ten minutes and was already changed.

"Ah, no. I'm going to the spa."

"Okay, I'm going golfing."

Hanni gathered some clothes from her suitcase and went back to the bathroom. She suddenly popped her

119

head back out. "Why are you going golfing? Do you even golf?"

"I have once or twice. It was mostly drinking and hitting things with a club Happy Gilmore style though." Chrys shoved the bill receipt in the front pocket of her jeans.

"Then why're you going? Maybe they have a massage spot open." Hanni smiled before disappearing again into the bathroom. It made Chrys want to puke. Hanni being nice was like the scorpion being nice to the frog so that he could get a ride across the river. Then before they get to the other side the scorpion stings the frog forcing them both to drown. His only excuse, "it's my nature." Hanni might be nice for the moment, however it was in her nature to sting. Curse her inevitable betrayal.

"I have to talk to someone about Tessa."

"Shouldn't you wait for your brother? You don't want to get your ass kicked."

"It was you who got her ass kicked," Chrys stated. "And don't you worry about me. Just go get your rub down and love yourself." Chrys meant the "go fuck yourself" version of love yourself, but Hanni probably didn't get it.

Chrys spent an hour and a half sitting in the parking lot at The Valley. Hadley's note said she should talk to Tessa's roommate, Louise, who was a beer-cart girl. After the first 30 minutes, she drove to the grocery store in the village for a bottle of water and a tray of cut-up fruit. She was pissed at herself for not having any type of plan. From what she knew, the beer-cart girl loaded her golf cart in the morning and drove around the course selling beer and vodka coolers to the golfers. Common sense said she would have to return to the clubhouse regularly to cash in and restock her coolers with drinks and ice. The few times Chrys had gone golfing with friends she learned how much people could consume while playing the "sport." Something about it begged people to drink. Today was a gorgeous day, the parking lot was at least two-thirds full. There had to be a lot of drinking going on. One of her last times on the links so many drinks had been downed by everyone in the party that they stripped down and went skinny dipping in a water hazard. That's why Chrys Alcrest was now banned from the Middleton Municipal Golf Course.

She didn't know when Louise had last been to the club house. What if she had returned while Chrys was at the store? What if she wasn't working? Chrys had searched her name on Facebook where she found 116 Louise Chambers'. She eliminated any who lived overseas, didn't have a picture or were not in the right age group. That cut it down, but still left quite a few. She searched the Fontana Hot Springs page with the woman's name and found only one that listed she was working there.

She didn't see Jonas either. She could see the kitchen door from where she had the car parked. A few cooks had come out to smoke cigarettes, but he wasn't one of them. She didn't know if he smoked. He was at the bar last night, so maybe he wasn't working today. Perhaps he had already worked the morning.

Chrys made herself more comfortable on the car seat. The watermelon and grapes were gone. She wasn't a fan of the pineapple.

She sat up when she saw a golf cart drive around the building to the kitchen door. It had a hard-top roof and two red coolers strapped to the back. The driver had long brown hair that was strung through the open space in the back of a ball cap and she wore capris with a resort golf shirt. Chrys only caught a brief glimpse before the girl disappeared through the kitchen door. Now what?

After a few minutes Chrys got out of the car. The fresh air felt nice on her skin. The inside of the car, even with the window open, was getting stale. She walked toward the back of the club house with the plan to talk to Louise when she came out. She wasn't sure what she'd say or ask, but she'd come up with something.

The door opened. Louise was there.

Chrys quickened her pace. Someone else exited the door. Jonas.

Chrys' foot slipped on a rock as her body twisted. Her hands hit the hood of a car as she dropped. She scrambled until she was beside the car door. Did Jonas see her? Did they hear her? Chrys got down on her hands and knees and looked under the car. She couldn't see any feet. There were still a couple of cars between her and open space, so maybe they didn't see or hear her.

In a squat she moved to the front of the car and peered around. She couldn't see the golf cart or either of the people. She moved a couple of cars back from the clubhouse staying on her haunches then slowly stood up and walked normally. Glancing over her shoulder she saw that nobody was there. The cart was still parked by the kitchen door, but Jonas and Louise were gone.

At the car Chrys sat for a few minutes with the door open and her feet still on the ground. One palm was scratched. Louise was outside the kitchen door now climbing into the cart and getting ready to go back onto the course. Jonas was nowhere in sight, but Chrys had already been too close to him seeing and maybe recognizing her. Who knew what he would do. The guy was nuts. She would have to find another way to talk to Tessa's former roommate.

Chrys had five messages on her phone. Three were from home. One was from Hanni asking where the hell her car was. The last was from her brother asking if she was keeping out of trouble. She didn't answer any of them.

Chapter 10

By 3:00 pm (around the same time Chrys was diving behind a car at The Valley) Spencer's tequila headache was easing. By 8:00 pm when Amam walked out the door the headache walked with him. He had tomorrow off and Amam was off the day after that. Two days without the walking wall of Egyptian tension. Spencer's shoulders seemed to relax at the thought.

"I hear you're a good singer," Bobbi was behind the kitchen line. Spencer told her she was doing all the cooking as soon as the chef d'partie left and he would be her dishwasher. They weren't that busy, so he wasn't worried about dishpan hands.

"Who said that?" Spencer leaned against the counter. He sipped Dr. Pepper from a yogurt container since he wouldn't allow glasses in the kitchen.

"Jenny, the server. She said you sang with some chick staying at the lodge."

"Yeah, Kevin picked up a couple." That was almost true.

"Anything happen with her?"

Yeah, something strange and mysterious that must never be mentioned again. "No. She was just using me for a singing partner. How come I didn't see you there?"

"We go to bed by eleven every night."

Spencer smiled at her. His dimples showed. "You're an old lady."

"I'm not that old. I like to party, just not with these people. My nights are for my boyfriend and me."

"What's wrong with these people?"

She shrugged her shoulders before wiping the counter with a wet cloth. "There are a lot of secrets around this place."

"Like what?"

"I don't know. They just seem to have secrets. People always seem to whisper together. I'm not in that group. Kevin and Jenny are. Becca, the booze-cart girl, is. My boyfriend doesn't work for the lodge, so we don't have to deal with any of it."

"What does he do?" Secrets? Kevin, Jenny, Becca…who else had secrets? Had he seen people talking with one another?

Bobbi adjusted the beanie on her head. A strand of mousy blond hair fell alongside her face. "Mike? He works construction. He works for the company building the new houses across the highway. They say they'll be building for years before the project is done."

"So you'll be stuck here for years?"

The order machine burst to life and spit out a printed bit of paper. Bobbi read it out before sticking the top into the chit holder. "Two cheese burgers with fries. One loaded nachos. No olives."

"Do you have that?" Spencer wasn't in the mood to cook simple food. He missed making up his own menu every day or two using whatever he found at the farmers or fish markets for inspiration.

Bobbi already had the insert container of raw hamburger patties out of the small fridge below the work station. "I'm good. Why do we have the Chinese menu if nobody orders from it?"

"And even the burgers are plain. They're seasoned, but still. At my place..." shit "...the place I used to work, we would make our own barbeque sauce and mix it in the meat."

"Oh cool." Bobbi stared at him a moment too long.

Spencer shrugged his shoulders and took another drink. "People thinking they know better when they really know nothing. Whoever decided on the menu, I mean."

Bobbi didn't speak again until all three plates were on the pass under the heat lamps and she rang the bell for the server. "They should get rid of it. Nobody orders from it."

The server, Sherry, came in and picked up all three plates. In this restaurant the servers kept to themselves in the dining room instead of spending half their time talking with the cooks like at home. It was a change from what Spencer was used to. The jury was out on which was better.

"Hey," he waited for Sherry to leave, "are there any sights to see around here?"

"The Hoodoos," Bobbi replied.

"I mean stuff not in the brochures. You've lived here a while, so you must know some places to hike to or whatever." He was working up to something.

Bobbi cleaned off the charbroiler with the wire brush. "There are abandoned mines. Almost like small ghost towns."

"Really?" He was pretty sure Tessa wasn't killed by a ghost. Possessed? Over his yogurt cup, he kept his eyes on Bobbi.

"Yeah they're all over. I can see if Mike can take you some time."

"There are none I can hike to?"

Bobbi shook her head. "The closest one is up the hill past the ski hill, but the road is overgrown and the road to the ski hill is closed anyway, so the next mining town is a good hour drive through back roads."

"Why is that?" According to his sister that was the direction Tessa had gone into the hills between the main resort and the ski hill.

"I don't know. Renovations or something."

The printer burst to life spitting out a long list of orders. Spencer took a large swig of Dr. Pepper before stepping behind the line. He instantly took charge telling Bobbi what he needed from her and getting out what he was going to cook. Of course the one table that ordered from the Chinese menu also ordered from the other menu. Szechwan beef with Chinese vegetables on soy-sesame Shanghai noodles next to a cheeseburger and poutine just did not seem right. To him it was like going to a Gordon Ramsay restaurant and ordering a bologna sandwich. They went through the steps preparing all the items, being sure to have them all ready at the same time.

As Sherry came to get the last plate of food Spencer snapped. "Next time we get a huge table, do you want to give us a heads up?"

She looked at him with a snarl on her lip and left the room with her nose in the air. At The Alcrest there might have been a snarl, however there also would have been a "Yes Chef."

"Can I ask you something?" Spencer had walked Bobbi out the back door when the restaurant was closed and the kitchen cleaned. His eyes locked on the spot where the staff trailers had been. "Do you know anything about the girl who killed herself?"

Bobbi looked toward the road. Mike picked her up every night. "Not much. She worked up at the lounge, so I never met her."

Spencer nodded. "What's the word about it? I mean did she really kill herself or was there foul play?"

She looked past where the trailers had been to the maintenance sheds. "Why are you asking?"

"Just curious." He smiled. The one thing he was confident about was his smile. His dimples showed. "It was a big question back home. The family was trying to raise questions or something."

A blue pick-up loaded down in the back with tools crossed the empty parking lot and stopped in front of them. Spencer had been introduced to Mike on his first night working with Bobbi. "How's it going Chef?" Mike was a nice guy whose hands always seemed to be dirty.

Spencer grinned and dropped his eyes. "I'm not the chef."

"That's what she calls you."

Bobbi climbed in the truck. "Spencer's curious about the girl who died."

With a friendly expression, Mike commented, "You know what they said curiosity did to the cat, eh? Around here we stay out of things."

Spencer kept his gaze on the other man's eyes. Was this guy involved with Tessa's death? Curiosity killed the cat. Was that just a threat or a warning?

"He's curious about the mines too. I said you could take him some time."

"Oh for sure." Mike's hair was thin enough to see his scalp. He was older than Bobbi by probably ten years and the lines on the sides of his face made him look even older. He had a leathery tan from working construction outside under the sun. "You have to be careful up there. One step in the wrong place and…" his hand slammed the dashboard. "They'd never find ya." He laughed.

Spencer tried to laugh. Did he just get threatened again? "Are there any you can hike to? Up above the lodge maybe?"

Mike shook his head. "There is one, but it would be a long-assed hike. I know there are a few hunting cabins up that way. I'll take you for a drive to see an old mine. This one looks like people just dropped everything and walked away."

"Yeah, that would be interesting." What the hell did Tessa stumble into?

~ * ~

For the twenty-third time Spencer looked over his shoulder. He knew from walking down to hill every night that the valley was always quiet at night and he could hear a car long before it got to him, but he still had to look behind him for a blue truck. He didn't know what to believe any more. Secrets being told. Was the curious line a threat? Either way he was walking faster than the night before.

At the corner where he'd met Chrys, he saw taillights from a car. The lights were also on in the brown house across the street. Inside a second floor window, dark curtains hung, but a sliver of light could be seen. He kept his eyes on the house as he approached the passenger door and slipped inside. "What are you…"

Hands grabbed him from the back seat.

Spencer yelled. He jumped out of the car, his feet slipping on gravel. His pulse soared. Pain shot from the old wounds in his body and he growled. "Fuck!"

He looked up at the window across the street. The curtains didn't move. He forced himself to take a deep breath.

In the dim light of the car's internal light Spencer gazed at bare legs beneath shorts in the driver seat. They were thin and pale, not muscular and caramel like his sister's. He bent down, his hands grasping the door and roof of the car as his knees felt week. The blond woman in the driver's seat smiled at him with a wickedness to her lips. Chrys leaned through the two front seats from the back. Her hair draped down.

"What the hell?" was all Spencer could say.

"Sorry, Spence." Chrys said she was sorry but her face said she was struggling not to burst out laughing. She had been jumping out at her big brother and scaring him their whole life. "Hanni insisted on driving."

132

He looked up and caught the curtains swaying. Spencer carefully lowered himself into the car (grinding his teeth at the twitches from the healing wounds) and shut the door. "Why are you even here? You can text me you know? Drive before someone sees us."

"Make up your mind." Hanni put the car in gear. "Who's going to see us? You two live in a fantasy world. Nobody cares about what you're doing."

Chrys fell back in her seat. "They killed Tessa. They may not know what we're doing yet, but they will."

"Oh please, she killed herself."

"She had cuts on her body, stab wounds." Chrys was back between the seats again. "So, what? She cut herself, got all bloody and then said "fuck it" and strung herself up? Who would do that? Nobody would do that. Maybe you would when you're high, but no normal person would."

Hanni twisted her face. She never admitted to using drugs, but everyone knew. Either that or she had the longest case of the sniffles in world history. "You're seeing what you want to see."

"Go across the highway. Are you hearing this, Spence?"

He stared out the window at the trees and houses going by. As they crossed to The Valley side of the highway, he let his eyes lock on new sites. What

133

Hanni said made him angry; however, she was right. The police said it was suicide and they didn't have anything that said otherwise.

"I might have a suspect." Spencer told them about his conversation with Mike.

"That doesn't mean anything." Hanni had a point.

"I don't think he did anything, but we can't rule it out, right?"

"I had a good day too," Chrys said then told them about the note from the server and her chat with the front-desk clerk. "That's a few people who said not to go up behind the lodge. I say we go up there tomorrow."

"I'm not going hiking."

Chrys stared at Hanni in the rear-view mirror. "Who the fuck invited you? Spencer?"

He still watched what was going on outside. They had gone through the entire Valley and were now heading to Kenora Lake. "Yeah, we'll go before lunch. I can meet you by the Indian bathhouse."

Chrys pulled herself up between them and propped herself against Hanni's seat. "And we have to talk to Louise. That server Hayden said she would know more about Tessa. We have to talk to her. I tried getting to her but Jonas got in the way. Oh, I know where Jonas works."

Hanni flipped her hair making it hit Chrys in the face. "You two are going to get yourselves arrested."

Chapter 11

Chrys ran a hand over the rough wall of the Indian bathhouse. She had a hard time imagining her own ancestors building and using this hut. She wasn't 100% certain what Aboriginal band she belonged to, but was pretty sure her people didn't sit around and soak. The walls were rock with a mortar made from the natural clay found all over the valley. It was a rectangular structure with three open doorways going into three individual rooms. On the floor of each was a rectangular hole in the rock that really looked like a bathtub. Each had been modernized with a tube and a tap to let the natural hot spring flow in if anyone wanted to soak here. She wondered if anyone actually used these. Two had cigarette butts in them and there was a pretty big spider web in a corner of one room. She used the digital camera hanging from her neck to take a few photos of the structure, leaving out the cigarette butts.

The sound of feet scraping against rock made her freeze. She had stepped inside one of the small rooms. Chrys quickly realized she had nowhere to go. There was an open window in each room, but that wouldn't get her far.

"Chrys." The voice was hoarse as if it was trying to yell out and whisper at the same time.

She stepped out of the middle room to see her brother standing by the first doorway. "You fucking scared me."

"Payback bitch!" Spencer got a punch in his arm for that one.

From the flat, moss-covered rocks around the bathhouse, they had an amazing view of the valley and the mountain range on the far side. It was enough of a view that it could not all be captured in one picture. Chrys stopped to focus her camera on the panoramic view as her brother quickly moved into the woods. At an opening in the trees was a pole with a wooden arrow pointing; it read Hillside Trail. Beneath it was a poster was stapled to the pole warning about cougars. Spencer looked over his shoulder. They had been out in the open since leaving the bathhouse. He couldn't see anyone, however had an overwhelming feeling of being watched.

As soon as they crossed into the trees they both slowed their pace. Spencer had his backpack slung over his shoulder. He had emptied it out in his room and only took what he thought they might need during a day hike. Dad always told him to have toilet paper when he went out, so there was a half roll in one pocket. He had thrown in his pocket knife and a spare t-shirt. He walked to the grocery store in the town for sandwiches, a couple pieces of fruit and two bottles of water. He noticed that his sister didn't have anything.

"What are you wearing?"

Chrys stopped and looked down her body. "What?"

"You're in your heels."

"So? They're boots." Her ankle boots had a three inch heel. "What's wrong with boots? You're wearing running shoes. We're not doing any running are we? And what's wrong with the rest of my clothes?" She wore tight charcoal yoga pants that flared out at the bottom and a black tank-top. She had a long sleeve shirt tied around her waist. "You're wearing chef pants and a sweatshirt. How is that any better?"

It wasn't really. "Did you bring anything to eat or drink?"

Chrys wiggled her travel bottle in his face, turned and marched down the trail ahead of him. Her boots crunched on branches and plants in the path. Okay, she didn't think about food, but she wasn't planning to spend all day in the woods either. She swatted a bug away from her face.

"Any idea where we're going?"

Chrys spun around catching her brother off guard. "How am I supposed to know?"

"I thought you said from her letter or journal you knew where Tessa went." Spencer slapped a mosquito against his neck.

"Doesn't mean I know everything. I know she took this trail and followed it until she came to a bridge. After that she basically stopped writing."

Spencer ran a hand through his blond hair. "Great, we're looking for Terabithia."

Every once in a while they heard a transport truck zoom down the highway far below, but otherwise they heard very little of modern society. The forest was pure Canadian; pine, spruce, birch and aspens. The trail was clear but not worn. There were ruts on either side indicating that a four wheel ATV had gone through on numerous occasions. People probably used these trails for hunting in the autumn. Surrounding them was an amazing painter's pallet of green. Little animals scurried in the underbrush. In other circumstances the forest would have been lovely.

A sudden sound stopped them in their tracks. Four deer walked amongst a grove of poplar trees snacking on the sweet-tasting shrubbery. The animals looked up at the trespassers and didn't seem to care that they were there. Chrys quickly snapped a few photos.

It took almost an hour before they reached something which might be considered a bridge. The trail split in two, the path on the left with a wooden bridge over a small creek. The main trail turned right until it disappeared in the same direction they had just come but a little higher in elevation.

"Her letter said she thought if there was a bridge it must lead somewhere." Chrys walked on across the bridge. "This is the yellow trail on the hiking map."

Spencer heard an engine, but wasn't sure where it was coming from. The sound seemed to echo in every direction. It wasn't a car or truck and it wasn't down on the highway. They had been moving upward along the mountainside. They hadn't heard anything from the highway for a while. This engine noise was something smaller, but powerful. Whatever it was, it sounded far away.

After crossing the bridge they found a trail ascending (Tessa's letter said she went up) that had been eroded by flowing water. The path changed from flattened grass to grass and ferns reaching up to their knees. The only parts which were flattened were ATV tracks. They could look up at the tree tops swaying the wind, but all they felt was the sticky heat of the day, even in the shade. Mosquitoes buzzed constantly around their bodies. Neither had thought to bring bug spray. Every twenty yards or so, a "No Trespassing" sign was nailed to a tree on one side of the trail. Once in a while they heard something rustling in the underbrush or in the branches over their heads.

"Okay, Chrys, how long are we going to walk before we decide we're not getting anywhere? We don't know what we're looking for. We don't know where Tessa went. Maybe hiking had nothing to do with it. Maybe she saw something when she was walking home."

"Then why no pictures? She took a couple of her hike and then nothing." They stopped walking. The path ahead turned to the left. Every time they turned a corner the path in front of them looked the same as what was behind. The hill sloped down on their right side and went upward on the left with small pine trees hanging over the edge above their heads. They couldn't see much around them except for the trees. They knew the mountains rose somewhere ahead and to their left, but the forest was too thick. Chrys wasn't sure herself if they were even still on the same mountain they had started on.

"Maybe her battery died." Spencer took out a water bottle, unscrewed the top and offered it to his sister before a healthy drink himself. He checked over his shoulder.

"Then how did she get the picture of her collapsed in her bed?"

"Plugged her camera or phone in?" The facial expression he gave her made his sister come back with a "Fuck you."

"Where do you think we are?" Chrys scratched a mosquito bite on her arm. She checked her phone. The last time she used it she had forgotten to turn it off and her battery was almost dead.

"I think the ski hill is in that direction." He pointed toward the corner. "We can go off the trail and head for the ski hill or we can head back or we keep going on the trail." It had been winding its way up the mountain back and forth the whole way. He honestly wasn't certain about which way they needed to go.

"Where would Tessa have gone?"

"I don't know." Spencer could still hear an engine noise. He was pretty sure it was somewhere behind them though and he repeatedly looked over his shoulder. Wherever it was, it was getting closer. He looked ahead through the trees hoping to see something so that he was certain where he was. When he was a teenager he was pretty good at detecting direction, but that was a long time ago in woods that he knew well.

"Let's just go then." Chrys marched forward again taking charge. Her heel came down on a root and her ankle twitched. She felt some pain, but didn't let on. She couldn't let her brother know what happened. All he would do is bitch about how he told her so.

"What's that sound? Is that an engine?"

"I think it's an ATV." Spencer looked through the trees in the downhill direction. He wasn't certain why. The sound was constant and getting louder.

"Good. Maybe they can tell us which way to go." She winced and moaned.

"You sprained your ankle didn't you?"

"I'm fine, Spence." She limped on. It was the same ankle she had hurt yesterday. She swatted wildly at mosquitoes. "Leave me alone." Her body was covered in sweat, her ankle hurt, her feet hurt, she was hungry, she itched all over, her tattoo throbbed...the last thing she needed was her brother in her ear.

Spencer shook his head. Something ahead and off to the side suddenly caught his eye. He stepped off the trail between two poplars and through the trees beyond that. If it was what he thought it was they were saved. "Chrys." He put his foot on one tree and pushed himself up higher. "Chrys, stop."

The forest was quiet.

She stomped her foot on the ground and let out a frustrated yawp. "What?" Chrys spun around and looked for her brother. She took a couple steps before seeing him on the edge of the trail. His body was almost hidden behind a tree. She glanced the way they had come. Her breath caught. Her heart seemed to pound through giant speakers right inside her ears and her legs wanted to let go. "Spence!"

Chrys froze. The rifle bullet cracked through the air beside her and a burning instantly soared through her body as if she'd been touched with a searing hot pan. Her whole body spun. Her knees gave out as she twisted and dropped to the ground.

She had to move.

Her heels tried to get grip on the ground. Her eyes were wide, staring at the canopy. *What was going on?*

Was she just shot? Chrys wouldn't let her gaze fall on her arm. *Where was Spencer? Who shot her? Where was he?* Her heart raced. Her fingers clawed at the ground. She had to get up. She had to get away.

Spencer looked over his shoulder. He saw the rifle trying to get a bead on him. There was no person behind it. All he saw was the long barrel of a gun.

He jumped down from the poplars and sprawled his body on the ground. His face hit something wet. He heard the bullet strike one of the trees he had just been between. The sonic crack seemed to explode and echo through the forest. He had to move. He had to find his sister. In the next instant he was on his feet. His mind spun as if it were trying to solve a problem. It was like a Saturday night and the restaurant was suddenly full. Just get the job done.

"Chrys?"

"Spence!" Chrys had somehow gotten to her feet. Something wet ran down her arm. Branches snatched at her clothes as she pushed through a grove away from the trail. One large branch hit her arm sending searing pain to her brain. She stumbled. Both her hands flew out. The left arm crumbled. Her face skidded across the damp ground.

An engine revved to life.

Spencer ran through the brush. Trees slapped against his skin. The engine was close by. It was getting closer. It was coming down the trail. "Chrys!"

Chrys' fingers grasped a sapling as she struggled to get up. Her body ached. Her arm was going numb. All she heard was the unnatural sound of an engine getting louder. And her brother. "Spence! Here!" She forced herself to sit up. She couldn't seem to blink.

"Chrys, I'm here."

Spencer stood in front of her, his face all muddy. When did that happen?

"Chrys, you with me?" He didn't wait for an answer. Her left upper arm was a mixed blend of crimson and black mud. He grabbed the other arm and pulled her to her feet. "We have to go."

What he had seen was shiny. The trees seemed to drop and beyond that was a metallic surface. He caught a glimpse of something, couldn't get a second view of it, but he was certain he had seen something in that direction.

Their feet scrambled over the ground. As Spencer jumped over fallen logs, Chrys almost tripped and he had to catch her. Her legs seemed to be a few seconds behind her brain. Branches stung their bare skin.

Ahead of them the ground gave way. It just dropped as if the mountain fell apart. Spencer's eyes searched quickly for a path downward. There had to be something. Some animal had to have gone down there. All there was were trees with witch's finger branches waiting to grab them.

Trees snapped behind them. The ATV engine roared as it dove off the path.

Chrys took the leap. With both feet, she over the edge. Her brother's hands were still hanging onto her arm and he lurched after her. Her feet caught up to her brain as she began to run down the hill. Spencer let go as he twisted around a tree. They ran quickly, jumped over logs and rocks, and continued running. They literally bounced off trees. Something cracked through the air between them. Chrys' foot caught another root and she pitched forward. Her body twisted in mid-air her left shoulder slammed into the ground. She summersaulted and was back up and running.

He aimed for a tree. His muscles tightened. His body struck the tree sending shots of electricity through his muscles making them want to seize. A scream left him. This was worse than the pain from two months ago. He turned to see his sister come to a slow controlled stop. The heels of her boots dug into the soft ground. As her body swayed, she grabbed a tree to steady herself. Her face was pale. Pine needles, leaves and dirt clung to the open wound on her arm and to her hair.

"Somebody fucking shot me, Spence. Who the hell was that?"

"I don't know." He looked back the way they had just come. It was a steep slope covered in trees both old and young. He had no idea how they were able to get down without falling and breaking bones on trees or rocks.

Spencer turned slowly, his eyes seeing everything and focusing on nothing. The slope they came down had a twin going up another mountainside. He tracked it up and down. It was a gully carved into the hills by years and years of water washing through solid rock. "We have to go. We have to move."

Both forgot their pain and took off running into the thicker brush. Water flowed at the bottom of the gully soaking through their shoes. Spencer realized they were heading away from the shiny thing he had seen, but they didn't have much of a choice. It was run or get shot.

Chapter 12

"My shoes are ruined," Chrys said pretty much to herself. Her face was pale and was covered in sweat. It was no *woman glistening* thing - this was pure dirty sweat. She stared down at her ankle boots which were half buried in the swampy ground. She raised her head and stared outward. "And I've been shot."

"It's barely a graze." Spencer pulled the tourniquet he had cut from his spare shirt tight around Chrys' arm making her wince. The bullet had cut a line across her arm tearing skin and flesh enough to make it bleed like she had been stabbed. Spence knew all about that. Unless they didn't get it treated she would live.

She looked at him with an expression of derision. "It was done by a bullet. It hurts like fuck! I've been shot!" There was the sister he loved. Dry blood and mud was caked to her arm and down the side of her body. "Do you think it's the same guy who got Tessa?"

"I don't know." Spencer looked back the way they had come. Since running down the steep slope they hadn't heard anything else except the faint ATV engine fade away. They had been crashing through the thick brush and splashing through swampy earth for over an hour.

For lack of a better way to describe it, they were between two mountains. The gully, which had probably once been a glacial river, rose steeply on both sides with thick enough brush and trees that they couldn't see the top. They hoped that meant nobody up there could see them through the green foliage. The sun was behind a mountain, so it was getting gloomy. The stream they had to walk through was at times two feet across in stagnant puddles and at others barely there running beneath spongy moss at their feet. It must have still been glacial runoff from the ice capped mountains because it chilled right through them. If it had been part of the hot springs they would have been okay. The trees were sparser up above with plenty of room to maneuver. Down here where there was constant water the bushes and vegetation were taking over making forward movement difficult. Spencer was pretty sure they were moving away from Fontana. He guessed that if they turned and went the other way it would eventually slope down into the valley. As it was they were constantly moving upward at an ever increasing angle. The real issues were how they were going to get out of there and would the gunman be waiting for them when they did.

"Are you getting anything from your phone? I don't have any bars. Shit, my battery's almost dead."

"No, I don't have any service. Must be the mountains." Spencer took a sip from his water. "Do we have a plan?" He handed the bottle to his sister.

"I have to come up with a plan?" She splashed some on her face before taking a sip.

"Don't waste that. You're the one who had us do a Young Guns Two off the cliff and end up down here, so yeah, you have to come up with a plan." Spencer pointed back the way they'd come. "That way is the lodge."

"And psychos with guns."

"And psychos with guns. I saw tin or something shiny that way too, at least I'm pretty sure I did."

"So what's this way?" Chrys pointed ahead. From what they could see through the trees they were heading straight toward a mountain with a snow-cover peak.

Spencer replied, "The Yukon."

"Are you saying we should head back?" No matter which way Chrys looked the growth was thick and unwelcoming. She couldn't even tell where they had just been. All signs of their broken trail had vanished. The walls on either side seemed to be vertical. She didn't like the looks of any direction.

Chrys' stomach twisted. She took a few quick breaths. She couldn't tell Spencer she felt ill. "What if the shooter is some crazy mountain man that lives in a cabin and the shiny shit you saw was from his place. He could have all of his victims staked to the walls like trophies with two empty spots for us."

"If it was a mountain man he wouldn't have just grazed you." They both stopped to think about that.

"It's almost 4:00 pm. We have to figure something out." Chrys bit back her fear. It was creeping inside her like a spider crawling on an arm, its furry legs pricking her skin with petite wire-like hairs. Only this spider was inside her and growing with every step. When her brother was eighteen, she thirteen, he trained with the Middleton Search and Rescue team and learned all about forest survival, so Spencer knew what he was doing in the woods. But he looked more scared than she felt. His eyes said he didn't know what to do or where to go. That terrified Chrys. That and she realized he was holding onto his side where he hit the tree. He had been holding it for a while now.

He saw her looking at him and dropped his hand. "We should keep moving."

"And go where?"

Spencer looked around. All of his survival training was telling him to turn around and head back down the mountain. The memory of gunfire sounds screamed at him not to. "Up?"

Chrys turned to the tree-covered slope. She couldn't even see the actual sloped ground through the forest. "What do you mean up?"

"We came from that side. If this guy is after us he's still on that side. If we go up the other side we should be okay." Spencer headed into the brush carefully pushing branches out of the way. He kept his hand on the thin willow trees for his sister to take them instead of having them whip her in the face.

"How the fuck are we going to get up there?" She grabbed the branches and followed. "It's a fucking mountain, Spence." Her foot dropped into a pool of water deeper than her boot. She almost stumbled as she felt the icy water inside. "Are you serious? For fu..."

"Chrys! Quiet."

Spencer stared at his sister for a moment and she glared back at him like she wanted to blast him with profanity. They didn't know who shot at them or why. They didn't know where the gunman was. He could have been watching them at that very moment with his finger twitching over the trigger of his rifle. With every step they took water splashed and the sound echoed through the trees and up the rock faces. If they snapped a twig or branch Spencer cringed and held his breath as he waited for the sound of a gunshot. He was fairly certain no one had come down that cliff after them, nobody sane anyway. The fact that the two of them survived was a miracle in itself.

He wondered if someone was really out to kill them. Perhaps it was just a mistake. They might have thought the pair were deer or elk. He wasn't sure who he was trying to kid with this thought.

Whether they knew who the two of them were was another question. Hanni was down at the lodge. If they knew who Chrys was then they could get to their friend. And there was nothing Spencer could do about it.

Grasping trees and rocks the two of them pulled themselves up the side of the gully. The muscles in their legs burned, far worse than any workout. Though both were in good shape (Chrys had been a dancer her entire life and Spencer played all the sports when he was younger and worked out when he could) neither planned on climbing the side of a mountain. Their clothes were soaked in sweat. Chrys had been climbing using only one arm, the other numb where the bullet had torn through. That couldn't be good. Spencer stopped every dozen steps or so to squeeze his side with his hand. His sister tried not to notice until he was grabbing his side every few steps.

"Spence, it's getting dark." They had stopped for a moment to share a sip of water.

"Yeah, I know."

"Well what are we going to do? Are we spending the night out here? Hanni will report us missing,

154

right?" Even Chrys didn't believe it as she voiced it. Hanni will probably find someone to buy her dinner, then get drunk or stoned and not even realize the Alcrests were missing. In the morning she'd probably still forget and go to the hot spring pools. "Your co-workers will, right?"

"I'm not even due at work until 1:00 pm tomorrow. They won't start looking for me for an hour after that and I didn't tell anyone I was going hiking." He didn't know how much further he could go. The pain in his side vibrated through his body. He had to find somewhere they could rest and be safe. This mountainside wasn't leveling off like the other. He couldn't really see through the trees, but was sure they were higher than the place where they had leaped. "Let's keep going and see if we can find somewhere to spend the night."

"What about food?"

"Give me a break, Chrys."

"Screw you. We're here because of you, not me this time. I don't need to give you a fucking break. Where are you going?"

Spencer marched up the hill. A rock slipped from under his foot and he landed on his knees. His running shoes were ruined as he'd been walking all this time in water. He looked up, searching for something that could serve as shelter. They didn't have much in terms of tools or energy to build anything. It was going to be a night under the stars with each other and the mosquitoes for company. He needed something that would protect them from wind or from being seen by crazy gunmen while hopefully stopping the two of them from rolling back down the mountain in their sleep, if they slept. They were lucky so far in that no clouds had rolled in meaning it would probably be a clear night. Thirty feet to the right an evergreen had fallen over, probably because it grew too big for the root structure to hold. Either way it had fallen to the side and still had green bows keeping the trunk off the ground. It was a natural lean-to, not perfect, but with a little effort he could break off some of the branches on the upward slope to use for more cover on the downhill slope.

After forty-five minutes they had a suitable shelter and some bows for the ground. It wasn't pretty, but it would do.

"What about a fire?" Chrys slipped off one of her boots. No water came pouring out like you'd have seen in the movies. It had all soaked into her foot.

Spencer sat beside her. The bows stopped some of the dampness, however they were extremely uncomfortable. "Do you have matches or anything?" She shook her head. "Me neither."

"Don't you have some "bush survival start a fire with two sticks" magic?" Chrys tried to smile, but didn't feel up to it.

"No. I don't know if we should have one anyway. A fire is easy to spot in the dark. They could start shooting blankly at the light."

"Oh come on." Chrys pushed herself up to her knees. She lifted her head above the fallen tree just high enough so that she could see over it. There was still daylight touching the higher mountains and trees, but where they were it was getting consistently darker. There was no way she would be able to see anyone across the gully without shining a light. She sat back down and hugged her knees into her body.

"Sorry about this," Spencer said as he rubbed his cold wet feet.

"Why? Did I apologize when I almost got you killed? I'm hungry."

"I have one sandwich left."

Chrys tightened the grip on her legs. "You can eat it."

"Maybe we should share half. Save the other half for tomorrow." He took the sandwich out. It was three slices of black forest ham and a slice of process cheese between whole wheat bread.

"You eat it."

"We share it or you eat it. Those are the only choices." Spencer held half a sandwich out for his sister. He had to wiggle it around before she took it and he could reseal the other half.

Chrys split it in half, handed one piece to her brother and took a tiny bite. "What? No mayo? And you left the crust on." She took another nibble and looked around. Their backs were to the downward slope, which wasn't that steep. No animals had come near them yet, but something could be heard scrambling around. "Do you remember how mom had those huge cookie cutters? I'd get dinosaur and bear-shaped sandwiches."

"She didn't do that for me. I ate everything when I was a kid." Spencer finished his quarter of a sandwich in two bites. "We don't have much water left. Tomorrow we have to try getting to the valley."

"What about the shooter?"

Spencer shrugged his shoulders. "He hasn't found us yet. If we stick to the cover of the mountain side we should be able to get to the ski hill first, then the valley, assuming this slope goes the whole way."

They sat quietly for a long time. The darkness of night crept over them. All they could hear was each other's breathing and the woods around them coming alive as creatures got used to the intrusion. There was a squirrel digging around somewhere. A few birds started to call from the trees. The mosquitoes never stopped their bombing. Both Chrys and Spencer had stopped swatting at them and let the tiny creatures do their thing.

Chrys lifted one arm so that she could scratch the back of her shoulder.

"Tattoo itchy?" Spencer smiled at his sister's wide-eyed look. "When I got my first one I rubbed it on every surface I could find. I'd rub it on the person sitting next to me sometimes, usually it was Tessa."

"So, you were rubbing Tessa in cooking school?"

"It was her idea for all of us to get tattoos, so she had to pay the price."

Spencer dug at the ground with a stick.

"What's with that weird grin? You're thinking about her aren't you?"

"No."

Chrys' mouth dropped. "You guys did something didn't you? You guys date or screw?"

"Neither." Spencer felt his cheeks get warm. He couldn't look at his sister. His thoughts were back in Prince Edward Island where he went to culinary school and to the things that went on there.

"Come on, brother. You have to tell me the story. What happened? You said you did nothing with her and your face is all red, so you better talk." She scooted over so that she was facing him.

He bit his lip. Spencer knew his sister was never going to let it go until he told her the whole story. Plus they had nothing else to do. "We went to Blooming Point beach. There was a whole group of us that went. It's a free beach so everyone goes there. It was packed that day."

"You fucked her on the beach! You dog."

"No. We hung out all day. We played volleyball and swam and built sand castles, drank some beers and had a good time. Then we were in the water. Tessa

159

and I were talking, I don't even remember what about, and we were pretty deep so we were hanging onto each other." He couldn't believe he was telling his sister this. Of course she had told him a lot worse. "It was getting too deep for her, so she wrapped her legs around me. I, ah, started to get excited. She said something about it, so there in the water at a full beach she pushed my shorts down a little, moved her bikini bottom and slipped, you know, me inside her. I kind of lifted her up and down until, you know."

Chrys slapped him with the back of her hand across his chest. "You fucking horn dog. Oh my God. I never thought you'd do something like that. What happened after?"

"Nothing." He flicked the stick away. "We never really talked about it again." He watched a leaf on the wind and thought of Tessa back when he really knew her. That really was it. They both cared about each other and became really good friends.

Chrys turned her body. "Can you scratch this?" She dropped the shoulder of her sweatshirt exposing her tattoo. There were thin scabs where the skin was healing.

"You shouldn't scratch it. You'll scratch off the scab then have blank spots on the flower. It is a nice design." He got close and blew air onto the tattoo. "So tell me about your new girlfriend."

"She's not my girlfriend. I don't even know if she likes me."

"Well, tell me something."

"What can I say? She's Australian and has a few tattoos. We've talked, but nothing more. I don't even know if she's noticed me."

"Then make her notice. You've been shot. You don't have time to waste. I've wasted my time on Jesse..."

"You think Jesse is a waste of time?" Chrys pulled her sweater close.

"I mean she and I don't know what's going on, so it's a waste of our time in a way." Spencer dug at the ground with a twig. "I just mean live life. Don't wait."

"Shit or get off the pot?" Her face was down, but her dark eyes turned up to him and she smiled. "Maybe you should listen to your own advice."

"Maybe."

"Can you look at my wound? It feels numb."

Spencer carefully unwrapped the piece of shirt he had wrapped around her wound. It had settled down. Any bleeding had long stopped and it was starting to dry and scab over. He had seen worse-looking kitchen accidents.

"It looks like you put your arm on an oven grate."

"How would I put my arm on an oven grate?"

"I don't know. That's what it looks like." He took a clean piece of the shirt and covered the wound.

They settled into their spots, almost leaning on each other, and tried to relax. They knew they probably wouldn't get much sleep with the mosquitoes and the cold. Their conversation steered in the direction that only a brother and sister stuck on the side of a mountain with an unknown gunman possibly hunting them could take it.

Spencer: "Super Mario Galaxy one is arguably the best Super Mario game ever."

Chrys: "Super Mario Three. Don't be a dick. Super Mario Three had different worlds, different powers, and different themes. It was just better."

Chrys: "Stupidest thing I've ever done? You remember that restaurant I worked at in Australia? The one on the pier? The chef dared me to jump out the window into the ocean, so I stripped to my chonies and took a flying leap. They told me later that there were sharks."

Spencer: "There are sharks all around Australia. For me it was taking help from an Irish mobster."

Chrys: "We've both done that."

Spencer: "I went vegan for a week once."

Chrys: "Eww, why?"

Spencer: "Temporary insanity. I guess my stupidest moment was driving out to Cam Markham's place out in the country the morning after a night of freezing rain rolling Dad's car."

Spencer: "Favorite Muppet?"

Chrys: "I liked the Dozers from Faggle Rock. Do they count as Muppets?"

Chrys: "I could go for some loaded nachos right now. Peppers, black olives, jalapeños, tomatoes, taco beef, bacon, sour cream, no green onion and extra cheese. Oh, and guacamole."

Spencer: "Flatbread pizza with basil pesto, a touch of tomato sauce, chicken, peppers, red onion, black olives and feta."

Chrys: "Oh that sounds good. I want that too."

Spencer: "And a pitcher of Dr. Pepper."

Chrys: "Ice water."

The only things they didn't talk about were Tessa and what they were going to do. Of course it was never far from their thoughts. At times during the night they both got quiet for long moments when those thoughts crept in. Somewhere during the night they both drifted off in restless bouts of sleep.

Chapter 13

"Breakfast is served."

Chrys looked up at her brother. She wasn't thinking about her tattoo anymore because her entire body itched from bug bites. She was one of those women usually lucky enough to wake up looking lovely. After a night on a mountainside she was anything but. Her cheeks were streaked with dirt. There was a nest of pine needles and twigs in her hair. "That's a handful of blueberries. I want a real breakfast. My mosquito bites that have mosquito bites have mosquito bites." To make their point a few buzzed into her ear.

"We'll get out of here today." Spencer's legs crumbled beneath him until he was sitting on the bows they had slept on. The needles were squished into the soft earth. His knees screamed at him.

"You're sure of that?"

He nodded. "I was able to see down the gully; pretty sure I saw our valley. We'll follow the mountainside all the way and get out. I saw something else too."

"What?"

"Eat first."

Without another word the two started popping blueberries in their mouths. Spencer kept count of them making sure his little sister had the bigger share. They shared the last of their water. Neither mentioned that there could be a hunter out there waiting for them to move. He could have already seen Spencer berry picking and was now in wait for the two of them to step out of their cover. They carefully unwrapped the bullet wound on Chrys' arm (if possible it looked even smaller than yesterday) and rewrapped it with the cleanest piece of shirt. As soon as they had everything gathered they started walking.

Spencer didn't say a word. He kept his eyes on his sister's and waited for her reaction. Ten minutes in they noticed the horizontal logs up ahead. A few seconds later she saw the windows and the roof covered in moss and dead leaves. A tiny tree struggled to grown on one corner of the roof.

"Are you fucking kidding me?"

"I found it while picking berries this morning. If we had kept walking last night we would have found it."

The cabin was small and well-hidden among the trees. It looked like it had been there a long time. One window pane was broken. The door was latched on the outside but had no lock in place. It appeared the cabin had been used in the recent past as there was a pile of firewood near the front door. Broken branches lay over what was once a fire-pit.

Chrys walked up to the door, flipped open the latch and opened it. For a split second she imagined the gunman being inside. He wasn't. The one room cabin was empty. In one corner was a cot structure but no mattress – just wood slats across it. In front of a table beneath the window stood chair made of solid branches nailed together. An old coat hung from a nail. On the windowsill there was a soup can holding dried wildflowers. On the table was a notebook with a stubby #2 pencil. She also found a rolled-up ball of socks, a pair of knitted mitts, a deck of playing cards and a matchbox with three wooden matches in it.

"I bet if you take something you're supposed to leave something. Bobbi told me about cabins in the woods." Spencer stood just inside the doorway. It felt nice to have the mosquitos stop for a moment.

Chrys fingered the notebook. She flipped to a random page and leaned in to read the faded words. "July 17, 2010. The anniversary of the greatest day of my life. So cool to find this oasis in the mountains. L and B. Beau wuz here 2007. This one is written in Spanish, I think." She turned each page and read what visitors had written. Her finger stopped on the last written page. "Spence, Tessa was here. She wrote, I got lost and found this place to regroup. Thank you to whoever put it here. Tessa K." Chrys looked at her brother. "We're on the right path. She was here."

Spencer took the book and read his friends words himself. She had been right there. What was she doing up here? Was someone chasing her? Did she get shot at too?

Chrys didn't like the look in her brother's eyes. "We should get going." She knew too well that memories could hurt even more than a gunshot wound.

This time it was Spencer's turn to get a flash of a movie scene. He felt if they stepped outside bullets would fly.

Today the sky was covered in white clouds with tints of grey. It wasn't as warm as it had been yesterday, but the sun hadn't reached over the mountains yet. Their legs were stressed with pain. As they continued along the slope their feet slipped, their empty stomachs groaned. Their clothes were damp with dew. After thirty minutes of walking the trees thinned out and they could see the other side of the gully and some of the valley ahead.

"If we keep up this pace, I might be able to get to work and nobody will know," Spencer said over his shoulder.

"Except the killer," Chrys yelled back.

"We don't even ..."

"What?"

Spencer clenched his fists at his side. He stopped walking and turned around so he wouldn't have to yell over his shoulder. "We don't know if the guy who shot at us has anything to do with Tessa."

"That's so much better." Her shoulders dropped. "There are two killers out there, much more comforting."

"What do you want me to say, Chrys? I know what you know."

"Fuck all?"

Spencer nodded and turned back to the trail. Chrys looked across the open gully and at the trees that grew below. She couldn't really see the bottom through the foliage. Something was out there. Something was watching them, or at least that's how she felt. It could have been a fox keeping an eye on the intruders in his world. It could be the green eye of a hunter looking through a mounted scope with his finger on the trigger. She took a deep breath then turned and followed her brother.

~ * ~

The cliff side sloped down as another mountain rose from behind. Halfway down they saw the bare ski slopes on the side of the mountain. The closer they got to the bottom the sound of running water made its way to them. They both knew the dangers of drinking "wild" water, however not having anything to drink all morning made them forget about that. Their pace quickened. As gravity took over they took two steps

and a little jump like a mountain goat in a Discovery
Channel show.

At the bottom of the slope, they encountered a
white shed, big enough to house a car. A stream of
water emerged from the far end of the shed through a
shoot joining water rising from the ground. It then
flowed over rocks and under a wooden bridge. A pipe
came from the shed heading toward the valley. It
disappeared under the ground. It was the pipeline that
brought the natural hot springs water down to the
lodge and the swimming pools. From inside they
heard the humming of machinery. The door appeared
to be thick metal with a strong lock on the
outside. The tin roof reflected the sun, it was hard to
look at.

"Maybe this was what I saw." Spencer waited for
his sister to catch up to him and they continued
walking.

"This is pretty far from where we tumbled."

"I don't know."

Across the bridge was a well-worn gravel road
leading away from the mountains and toward the
valley.

Chrys scrambled down to the water's edge. She
quickly splashed a few cupped handfuls onto her
face. To her brother's asking if it was cold or hot
water she replied with a simple, "Wet."

Spencer splashed a little of the naturally hot water
onto his face. Both tried not to drink much. It was

probably safe, however they could get extremely sick from drinking fresh water in the wild. "This road should take us to the ski hill and then down to the main lodge. I'll make it to work on time."

"I just want something to eat." Chrys groaned

They crossed the bridge and began up the road. It felt great to be on flat land instead of the slanted mountainside where one slip could kill them. The grass on either side had grown so high it curled over like breaking waves. An assortment of wildflowers created a lovely picture in the ditches and scented the air with their fragrance. This time bees, instead of mosquitoes, buzzed around them. There were more birds down here flitting in and out of the tree cover. The road appeared to be used frequently and no grass pushed through the packed clay and gravel tracks. Someone probably came to check on the pumps in the shed once or twice a day. He and Chrys could just sit and wait for whoever that was to come along, but they had no way of knowing when the last time the pumps had been checked or when the next check would take place. Except for Chrys rubbing her stomach and moaning, it was an easy walk.

After ten minutes the road opened to a wide gravel area. On the far side was a dark brown building made of wood and glass. It had an Alps feel with an extremely steep roof so snow would slide away. Behind it they saw signs of a chair lift rising up the cleared ski hills. It wasn't working now, but in the winter it probably rarely stopped. The cleared area in which they stood was likely the parking lot during ski season.

"There's an SUV over there." Chrys pointed to the ski lodge. They could see the back of a white SUV behind the building. "Someone might be over there." She broke into a jog.

Spencer didn't move. "Wait!"

Chrys' boots skidded on the gravel.

"Nobody is supposed to be up here. That might just be a parked truck or something else. Let's head down the road."

"But that might be someone." Her hands waved toward the lodge. What the hell was her brother doing?

"And it might be a waste of time. Let's head down the road." Something ached inside Spencer's chest. He had a bad feeling as well as feeling that someone was watching them.

"But look." She took a few more steps toward the lodge. "There's smoke coming out of it. Someone's in there."

That's what he was worried about. There was a strange smell in the air. "Let's go, Chrys. I'm serious."

"What the fuck, Spence?"

"Let's go."

Chrys threw up her arms, then slapped them against her thighs and stomped her feet as she headed toward the road. Her boots crunched on the ground.

Spencer kept one eye on the SUV as he followed her until it vanished behind the building. He had seen one like that recently with a security guard behind the steering wheel. That didn't mean that's who was there now, but it didn't mean it wasn't.

Their knees felt like they were soaking in gelatin. Since breakfast yesterday they had shared two sandwiches and a handful of blueberries. Their bodies screamed for nourishment. It was over twenty-four hours since they'd walked into the bush. The more steps they took the weaker their bodies felt.

Spencer checked his phone for service, but the battery was almost gone. No matter what he did he was going to be late for work. The first text went to his boss. He was somewhat honest. "I went hiking yesterday and got lost. I'm going to be late for my shift." The second text went to Hanni. "We're okay. Hope you didn't worry."

"There's a truck." They heard an engine change gears as it got closer to them. Chrys broke into a run, her feet pounding the ground. She waved her arms in the air. "Hey! Come on, Spence," she yelled over her shoulder.

He wanted to tell her to stop. They didn't know who might be driving it, but at this point, he didn't care anymore.

173

The truck turned the corner and came into view. It was a pick-up with a mural of the mountains painted on each side, which they saw when it pulled up beside them. Fontana Hot Springs was painted above each mural. The driver came to a stop and opened the window. Beach Boys music danced from the stereo. The woman inside flicked a ponytail over her shoulder. She took off her pink hard hat and ran a forearm over her sweaty brow.

"What are you two doing up here? This is a restricted area."

"We got lost," Chrys left out the details. "Can we get a ride?"

The woman squeezed her bright pink lips together bringing out the lines around them. She was older than the two of them, but had an air of confidence that came with the surfer music. "I'm supposed to check on the water pumps, but I guess I can drive yous down and come back. Get in, man. I'm Allison, with two ells. I hate it when someone spells it with one."

"I'm Chrys. This is Spencer." Both of them squished together in the passenger side of the bench seat. Chrys ended up sitting on a pair of work gloves. The inside of the truck smelled of cigarettes and engine oil – or maybe that was Allison.

"You guests at the lodge?" Allison asked after doing a three-point turn and heading down the hill.

"Yes."

Spencer didn't say a word. He kept his eyes on his phone waiting for an answer from Hanni. In his mind he went over all the reasons she wasn't answering.

"Oh, man, must suck to be lost on holiday. How long were yous out there?"

"Just a couple of ..." A vehicle came up the hill toward them. The dark grey SUV sped past and continued up toward the ski lodge. It sent up cloud of dust that enveloped the truck.

Spencer put his phone down and turned to watch the dust cloud through the back window. "I thought this road was restricted?"

"Yeah, man, for sure. That guy is the boss, so he goes wherever. Must be checking on the work up there."

"What are they doing?" Spencer settled back in his seat. There was still nothing on his phone.

"No idea. Renovations at the ski lodge I think. Not my business." She stopped the truck at the bottom of the road where a metal bar blocked entry. On the other side of it was a road that circled the main lodge and led to an RV park. On the opposite side of the road were tall manicured trees with the main lodge right behind them. "Do you guys mind walking from here? It's just a pain to get out and lift the bar every time."

"No problem. Get out, Spence. Thank you for the ride."

They walked around to the front doors of the lodge. Spencer bowed his head and raised his shoulders as they quickly passed through the lobby. They both looked like they had been through the ringer. He didn't want anyone to see they were together, but needed to see if Hanni was okay.

"I'm ordering room service then getting in the shower." Chrys used the railing to pull herself up the stairs.

"Chef texted me. He told me to come in whenever. Hanni hasn't answered."

"Probably in the pool. If she's in one of her skimpy bikinis just look for the group of men. Really, the woman has no curves, wears push up bras and is a bitch, so how does she get every dick's attention?"

"She has great legs." Spencer was glad he was walking behind his sister.

"Only when she's in heels."

"And she has confidence."

"You should eat before going to work."

"I'll get something." All he really wanted was a big jug of water. "Did that car look familiar?"

"What car?" Chrys slipped her room key out. She was surprised she still had the plastic card. After pushing the Do Not Disturb sign out of the way it took two tries to get the green light to flash on the door lock and for them to hear a click.

"That car on the road. That SUV that went up the hill. It looked expensive." Spencer followed his sister into the room. She instantly disappeared into the bathroom. The drapes were drawn, so the room was black except for slivers of light sneaking beneath them. Spencer's hand groped the wall for a second and found a light switch. The bulb in the ceiling bathed the room in light. Spencer blinked quickly. "Hanni? Hey, Hanni."

The woman lay face down on the bed, the blankets tossed onto the floor and the sheet scrunched up beneath her. She wore tight jeans, but no top. Her stiletto heels had been discarded at the end of the bed. Spencer stared at her bare back hoping to see some type of movement. Nothing. Her face was turned away from him with her blond hair covering it. Half her face was off the bed.

His eyes went to the tiny table between the two beds. There, beside the digital clock-radio was a glass pipe. Beside that was a tiny plastic bag. Spencer knew she put stuff up her nose, but the extent of her use he didn't know.

The voice in Spencer's head told him to check to see if she was alive. Did someone do something to her because he and Chrys were looking around? Did she do this on her own? How many families of his Alcrest staff would he have to talk to about their deaths?

"Hanni?" Spencer snapped out if it. He leapt over the corner of the bed. "Chrys, I need your help." He knelt beside Hanni. There was vomit on the floor under her face. He pushed back her hair. She moaned. Spencer stumbled back, fell and hit his back on the other bed.

"What the fuck?" Chrys jumped on the bed and gave the woman a good shake. She moaned again and mumbled, but none of the sounds actually meant anything. "What the hell did you take?" Chrys grasped Hanni's face with one hand. The blond woman opened her eyes for a second, but didn't see. The expression in her eyes was blank. "She's completely wasted."

"We have to wake her up." Spencer pushed his sister away and picked up Hanni in his arms. She barely ate anything normally, so even as dead weight she wasn't heavy. His sister helped to lower her into the bathtub.

"I'm calling for an ambulance," Chrys said. Her brother turned on the cold water in the tub and let it shower down on Hanni. It took almost five minutes before she came to. "They're going to be about thirty minutes." Chrys hung up the phone and called room service. She had them bring fruit, sandwiches and bottled water.

By the time room service arrived, Spencer had Hanni sitting in an arm chair wrapped in towels and a blanket. Her hair dripped. Her skin was almost white. She had trouble keeping her head up. She wouldn't answer when he asked what she had taken.

His shirt was soaked through and pants were damp. Spencer knelt beside her and slowly ran his hands through her hair. If asked he wouldn't have been able to explain what he felt for this woman. She flirted with him and tried to wreak havoc in his life, but there was still something unspoken between them. He would want to say it was sisterly, but he didn't look at his sister the way he looked at Hanni.

"Spence, what's this? I thought Hanni was a coke-head. This isn't cocaine." Chrys showed him the small Ziploc baggie from the bedside table.

Spencer took it and held it beneath the lamp. The pale green crystals inside glimmered under the light, a light green that you could almost see through. "I think this is crystal meth. It might be. Hanni, Hanni, what is this? Is this meth? Where did you get this?"

"How do you know what crystal meth looks like?" Chrys checked the time. The ambulance should be there any moment.

Spencer slipped the baggie in his pocket. "Jesse Pinkman is my favorite TV character."

Hanni moaned. "Where's Kevin?"

There was a knock at the door.

Chapter 14

"Where's Kevin?"

Amam came from the back prep room. "Where you been?"

"Don't start with me, Amam. Where's Kevin?" Spencer stared into the eyes of the Egyptian who stared right back. His hands were in tight fists and he was ready for a fight. Spencer had let the ambulance crew into the hotel room but slipped out before curious resort staff could see him. He took the cross-country path that led past where the old trailers had been and marched into The Pass kitchen. His clothes were still damp from the shower and he was covered in forest filth.

In a timid voice Bobbi said, "His shift was done an hour ago," then went back to washing dishes as soon as Amam's gaze fell on her.

"And you were supposed to be here two hours ago." Amam crossed his arms over his chest and tried to make himself appear bigger. During his first few days here, Spencer would have backed down, but not today.

The order machine chirped to life and spit out a ticket. Amam moved toward the kitchen.

Spencer put his hand out stopping him. "Bobbi, can you cook that."

"She doesn't know…"

Spencer glared at him. "She knows plenty. Bobbi, please."

Bobbi circled around to the hotline keeping her eyes on the tile floor. Spencer stepped aside so she could pass. Amam, however, didn't budge and she had to sidestep around him.

Both men stared at each other. Spencer knew this was a contest. They were both standing there measuring their cocks and the first one to flinch had the small one.

Spencer turned his eyes to the woman as she checked the order and started cooking. From the corner of his eye he saw Amam watching as well. As she put the last plate on the pass, the Egyptian grumbled something about having prep to do and walked to the back room.

"What was all that about?" Bobbi asked.

"What?"

Bobbi's mouth dropped. "You, ah, came in all crazy. You scared me."

"Sorry." Spencer slipped his chef jacket off a hook. "How was yesterday?"

"Fine. Why do you want Kevin?"

He didn't want to say. The true story would only reveal that Kevin wasn't who he was pretending to be. It was probably a good thing that Kevin had left before Spencer got there because Spencer would have said or done something he shouldn't have. Just thinking of Hanni when he first saw her on the bed and that he thought she was dead made his blood boil. She was part of his restaurant family. She meant something to him, what, he didn't know for sure.

He shrugged, said "It was nothing" and went into the washroom. After locking the door he leaned against the counter and stared at himself in the mirror. The man staring back wasn't the one he knew ten years ago when he knew Tessa. It sure wasn't the carefree one that was with her in the water at Blooming Point beach. He wouldn't know that man if he saw him today and he wasn't sure if that man would like this one. The young one was fearless, but that had changed. When his dad got sick, Spencer did his duty and took charge. He became sterner. He was more serious. He stopped with the tattoos and women and even drinking, for the most part. He didn't always like looking at himself now. He was becoming his dad and he knew what that meant. His girlfriend Jesse was part of that seriousness. The pregnancy scare just a short time ago was serious. He didn't like being serious. Shit, a woman he had sex with was dead. Hanni wasn't serious. That was why he liked her, why he fantasized. He needed a little of that in his life. Cooking and life were no longer an exciting game. No matter how much he didn't like the man looking back at him he didn't have a choice but to put up with him.

~ * ~

Chrys watched the cop from the corner of her eye as she found the exit at the end of the hallway. The RCMP officer was focused on the nurse he was talking to, Hanni's nurse. If she got a good enough jump, Chrys thought she could beat him to the door. She had changed into pajama pants and a sweatshirt before leaving the resort, so nothing but her soggy boots were keeping her back. Of course he did have a gun and she had no way of getting away once she was outside.

The ambulance brought them to the closest town Yanko where a two-story hospital serviced the area. Chrys told them Hanni overdosed on something, but didn't say what. She said she didn't know. It was mostly true.

One of the paramedics had seen her wrapped arm and asked what had happened. Chrys took a lesson from her brother and said she had burned it. When he started asking questions she took a lesson from Hanni and laid the flirt on pretty thick. You'd be surprised how cute a woman in lounge clothes could be. Especially when she stripped down to her sports bra so he could get a better look at her arm. She was proud of her body and happy to show it off. She wondered if it would work on the cop.

"Miss?" At least the RCMP officer was handsome.

"Chrys." She stood. Her whole body still felt icky from the night in the woods. Her hand automatically rubbed her arm where she had been shot.

"Miss," the officer repeated, "do you have any idea what drug your friend took?"

"I told them I didn't know."

He stared at her for a moment. His bushy eyebrows made him look serious. "I know you said that, Miss, but if you do know you need to tell us."

"I got to the room and found her passed out."

"And then you got her into the shower, by yourself?"

Chrys folded her arms in front of her. She flinched when her fingers touched her wound. She hoped he didn't notice. "With help from a hotel staff member. I didn't get his name. I yelled in the hallway for help and he came. After we got her out of the shower he said I should call an ambulance and left." She had been thinking about the story the whole time. It sounded good to her. Her brother did work for the resort, so it was true.

The officer wrote notes into his little book. "Did you see any small green crystals? Did you see any small baggies?"

"No, I didn't see anything. Do you know what it might have been?"

The officer looked at her for a while deciding if he should say anything. "We've found a drug out here called Emerald, it has a green tint. It's a new form of methamphetamine that we are finding in the mountains. Your friend is showing classic signs of an overdose."

"Well, like I said, I don't know what she took or if she even took anything. She could be sick for all I know." Chrys thought about the tiny baggie of green crystals in her brother's pocket. If he got caught with that everything would be screwed up. "Look, can she and I go? I was hiking all…morning and I need a shower."

"All morning? The nurse says the drugs were in your friend's system a lot longer than that. Were you with her this morning?"

Shit. "No. I shacked up with a guy last night." Oh yeah, quick thinking Chrysanthemum.

"Who was that?" The cop had his pen ready to write the name down. "What was his name?"

She lifted her shoulders. "Didn't get it."

The nurse snorted in scorn. "Your friend has to stay in observation until tomorrow anyway."

Hanni looked at them from the bed. She didn't say anything and her expression made it seem like she was barely there inside.

"I can leave, right?" Chrys looked at both of them. She still wasn't sure how she was going to get back to the lodge, but she didn't want to stay there.

~ * ~

The hat came off and Spencer ran his fingers went through his hair as he used his foot to open the back door to the restaurant and stepped out into the hot sun.

They were actually busy for once. The parking lot was full of expensive-looking vehicles, most with Alberta license plates. Being busy made you forget life. Unless, of course, you had to call for the mad Egyptian to help you out and tell the lady cook to go back to washing dishes. Amam didn't lose the smirk on his face for the seventy minutes they were busy. Spencer was used to his sous chef at The Alcrest who wouldn't talk while concentrating on the task but then would tell a joke as soon as they were done and they would all relax. This tall man finished his work then walked back to his prep area with only an "I told you so," glance at Bobbi.

Spencer wanted to know what was happening with Chrys and Hanni. His phone was dead. He hoped things were okay.

The sun's rays today were shining from the mountains. It was hard to believe that he spent a day and night running from a gunman and now he was sweating in a kitchen as if it were a normal day.

Spencer walked around the corner and leaned against the wall. He was exhausted. He had been drinking as much water as he could to rehydrate himself, but he still hadn't had enough.

His eyes dropped onto the drink cart parked on the other side of a foot-high fence with nobody in the seat or standing around. The only time the girls were supposed to leave the carts were to serve customers or refill their coolers. He pushed away from the wall and walked down the parking lot between rows of cars. Something was off; a knot grew in his chest. Over a nearby vehicle he saw the top of a head. Spencer didn't know what he was getting into, but felt the need to tiptoe and crouch down so as not to be seen. By the time he could see he was almost his knees.

A man and woman were standing between a minivan and a Porsche. The man was dressed in trousers and a golf shirt. His impressive golf bag stood beside him. Spencer could see the woman. She was young, in her twenties, and wore the uniform of the Fontana Resort. It was funny how even though Canadian labour laws said you couldn't hire people based on appearance all of the drink girls were good-looking, young and sexy. He didn't care about what she looked like. What he cared about was in her hands. She was looking through a stack of money, with her painted fingernails flipping through bills. She reached into the pouch on her hip and handed him something small. Spencer swore he saw the sun's rays bounce off of something green. It reminded him of the small package he had in his pocket.

~ * ~

It wasn't the first time in her life Chrys had to hitchhike. Being cute had its benefits. She was picked up within five minutes and driven directly to the front door of the lodge. She waved at the perky front desk clerk. The same woman who had helped her with the hiking map flashed a smile as she reached for the phone.

Hanni was fine at the hospital, for the moment. The police had nothing to charge her with and even if this Emerald drug was found in her system there was nothing they could do.

Chrys' plan for today was to have a long, hot shower with an extreme amount of shampoo and body wash, then try to talk to Louise again. And a nap. And food. She slid her room key into the lock daydreaming about room service.

"Excuse me."

The man's voice startled her. She was lost in dreams of a fruit platter and didn't hear the person behind her. Persons she realized as she turned to see the lady from the front desk, Blaire, and a tall man dressed in a security guard uniform. The name tag on his chest said he was Trent, Head of Security.

"Is this your room?"

Chrys looked at the woman standing almost behind the man. Her smile was gone and it looked like it hurt not to have it. "Yeah, why?"

"I'm afraid ma'am," Chrys preferred being called miss, "that because of recent events the resort management is requesting that you vacate the hotel and leave the property."

Chrys looked at him. His cold eyes stared back. She thought his tanned skin made him look older than he was. His shoulders were square and solid. In a different place and time she would gave him a second look. "You're serious? What events?"

"We have been told that the woman you are staying with had a drug overdose. We don't tolerate illegal substances at Fontana Lodge." His hands were on his hips as if he were the big man

"What illegal substances? Who the fuck told you this?" Her eyes moved between the two of them. Anger built up inside. She could feel her chest burning and was getting ready to blow. Where the hell were they going to stay? "There were no illegal whatever's involved in anything. She was sick."

"We have it on authority that your friend had an overdose," Blaire said. "We're here to watch as you pack your things. We can do it this way or call the police," she added.

"Bite me." Chrys thought about saying other words, but that wasn't going to do any good. Instead

190

she turned around and put her key card in the lock. The red light lit up. She tried again with the same result. "My key's not working."

"We know." Trent stepped up to the door and unlocked it with one swipe of his key card. With a smug expression he looked at Chrys as he pushed the door open and waited. He smelled of sweat and body odor and something else that she couldn't place. It was sweet and contrasted the other scents. Medicinal maybe. "After you."

"Really? You guys have to watch me? Am I going to steal the cheesy painting over the bed or the shower curtain?" Chrys stomped into her room like she did when she was little and forced to clean against her will. She thought about taking her time to fold everything neatly and placing each item one at a time in their luggage, but then she realized she had never folded anything in her life. Her room at home was a toxic dump of clothes and shoes. She took more care with her items than Hanni's, however. She couldn't believe how much clothing Hanni went through in just a few days. She must have changed four times a day.

She tossed the blankets to see if anything was in them before throwing them across the room. Both Trent and Blaire didn't move from the doorway. One or the other made a noise every time she moved something around and Chrys stopped to give them her best go-blow-yourself glare. When Chrys went into the bathroom she looked at the shower with longing. Her dream of a long, how shower would have to wait.

One last check around the room and she pulled the handles up on the suitcases and marched out of the room. The other two followed close behind as though they thought she was going to take off down another hallway and find a place to hide. That actually sounded like fun. She wondered how long it would take them to catch her. Chrys started to whistle.

At the front doors to the lodge she turned and yelled, "If she did OD on drugs she got them here." and walked out the door.

As she put the bags in Hanni's car she looked back at the lodge. Trent got into a white SUV but kept his eyes on her. She saw him light a cigarette. They were really serious about this drug thing. That or they were hiding something. But she had to find a place to stay before she could get into that.

~ * ~

Spencer smelled mowed grass as he walked down the hill. He really used to like that scent. He didn't get to sniff it much anymore. They didn't have a lawn at the restaurant/apartment. In his teen years his dad would buy homes to renovate and resell at a profit. Spencer hated the days he had to mow their lawns, mostly because he wasn't allowed to go to the restaurant to hang out with the cooks. As he got older and stressed with running the place he longed for those days of pushing a mower around. He shoved his hands into his pockets and breathed the scent in. Yeah, he would have to admit he enjoyed the walk down the hill and was going to miss it when this was all over. Not even what he saw at the bottom of the hill was going to ruin this mood. Not until he got there.

He didn't say anything until he was in the car. He'd seen it as he was walking away from the golf course parked where his sister and Hanni had met him before. He made sure to look up at the brown house before he got in. None of the other houses had a view of them. "What the hell Chrys?"

"What?" She turned down the radio. She had been listening to the all-female band The Wolfe. She felt like there was a wolf out there somewhere.

"What? I haven't heard from you all day. What's going on with Hanni?"

"Nothing. She's fine. I've been with her the last couple hours and she's all better…ish. New problem though."

Spencer knew his sister's voice. This one gave him that "sore neck, things are not good," feeling.

"We got kicked out of the lodge and aren't supposed to be on the property." She gave him a quick rundown of what happened. After she got kicked out of the lodge she drove back to Yanko and found a cheap hotel. It had a shower and that was all she cared about. Her shampooed hair filled the car interior with the scent of flowers.

"Trent was the one who warned me about the old staff trailers." Spencer stated.

Chrys nodded. "And he drives a white SUV. Remember we saw the back of one up at the ski lodge. Maybe he's involved in all this."

"We don't even know what all this is."

She drummed the steering wheel. Some of the houses around had display lights on the exteriors showing off their improvements. "You know the cop was very interested in what drugs Hanni took. He said Emerald is a big problem up here. You ever hear of it?"

"No. I thought I saw one of the drink girls selling some of it today though. I don't know for sure. I have to get my brain sorted out."

"Yeah, and I have an hour to drive to my hotel."

She pulled away from the curb and headed down the hill. Neither of them saw the curtains in the brown house sway.

Chapter 15

Chrys was fine with food, but she had run out of drinks. She'd tried a breakfast sandwich with coffee from a café in Yanko, but finished the sandwich quickly and concentrated on swallowing the murky brown liquid. She was now munching on cheesy Doritos that she dipped into a small tub of sour cream and was eyeing the homemade chocolate chip cookies she'd bought earlier. When this adventure was over she was going to have to hit the gym. She had just finished the bottle of water she had also picked up. An hour into her stake out and she had moved from the driver's to the passenger's side of the car. She had flipped her boots off and had her bare feet locked between the steering wheel and dashboard (her shoes had dried, but didn't feel right). She hadn't thought about what she would do if she had to rush out of the car. Her boots were ruined, but wearable. She really didn't understand how cops could do this all the time. Stakeouts had to be a TV and movie thing, because she could barely stay awake. And she had to pee.

She had seen some of the breakfast staff leave for the restaurants. She had parked as far from Birch Grove as she could and close to a camper so she would blend in while still having a good view of the two doors. Luckily the campsite was full for the weekend, so there were lots of vehicles. She saw Jonas leave for work before 6:00 am and walk across the highway to the valley side. It was surprising that he hadn't run into her brother yet, but Spencer said he didn't really see anyone and stayed in his room.

She tossed her jacket into the back seat leaving her in grey yoga pants and a sleeveless red blouse with a draped neckline, not proper stake out attire, but comfortable. Her hair was in a top knot to keep it off her neck.

She couldn't come up with a good solution to her pee problem. The store down the road was probably open, so she could jet down there and be back here in fifteen minutes but she might miss her quarry. The idea of popping a squat in the bushes occurred to her, however the same concern about missing her quarry came to mind and she only had one napkin from her sandwich to wipe with. Chrys could run into her brother's room and use his toilet. If she did that he would be pissed about her doing a stake-out.

She sat up quickly, groped for her boots all the while keeping her eyes on the woman who had just come out of the building. Chrys had seen Louise Chambers once before and she was certain this was her.

"Louise," Chrys called out as she ran across the parking lot.

As the young woman turned, her ponytail bounce. She didn't say anything.

"Hi." Chrys pasted a smile on her face. "I'm Chrys Parker." She had been practicing saying the name all morning, "a reporter from Middleton. Can I ask you something?"

The woman's scrunched up expression distorted the painting of freckles on her face. Her sandals kicked at the ground as she shuffled her feet. "What? Who are..." something seemed to register in her eyes, "I have to get to work."

"I want to ask you about Tessa," Chrys realized she wasn't sure how to say Tessa's last name, "your former roommate."

Louise looked around quickly. "I can't. I have to get to work."

"I can walk with you." Chrys wasn't planning to take no for an answer. She took a few steps in the direction the other woman had been going and waited.

"I don't think I should be..."

"You're not telling me anything you haven't told the police. Like, you said you found Tessa sharpening knives in the bathroom one morning, right?"

They both waited at the side of the highway for five vehicles to go by. Louise's face seemed to relax knowing that Chrys knew something, however her eyes still had a panicked look to them. "Yeah, so?" They quickly crossed the highway.

"When was this?"

"I don't know. It was a little while before she … she killed herself."

"Was it strange for her to do that?" Chrys wondered if she should have had a notebook and at least pretend to be taking notes.

Louise fixed the shoulder strap of her backpack. "I don't know. I heard her doing it a few times I guess. She said she didn't want to disturb me and needed the water."

"So it wasn't a one-time thing?"

"No. I probably shouldn't be talking about this." Louise nervously looked behind them. Her eyes were moist, she almost looked afraid.

The road they walked on separated the fourteenth fairway of The Valley course and a new housing development. The construction crews were in full swing. A bulldozer was clearing land and the sounds of nail-guns and saws echoed across the open area.

Chrys was losing her. "Tessa's family doesn't think she'd ever commit suicide. They don't think they've been told everything." She couldn't tell if she was getting to the young woman or not. She had one more shot to try and make a point. "I'm just trying to put their minds at ease, Louise. They blame you for a lot of what they've been told. They blame you for the lies." Chrys was almost yelling at her firstly, to be heard over the construction noises, but likely due to frustration.

Louise shuffled her feet on the paved road then stopped walking and turned to look at the other woman. Cars sped by on the highway. A transport truck seemed to make the ground shake. Conversation from people already on the course floated in the air. No sounds came from the young woman for a long time, however she absently wiped a tear from her cheek. "I didn't lie. I told the police what I saw and knew. Don't call me a liar."

"I'm not calling you a liar. I'm just … Tessa sharpened her knives in the bathroom?"

"Yes."

"She did it more than once though and had good reason for it?"

"I guess. She sharpened them at night once and I didn't like the sound the blade made on the stone."

"Was she depressed?"

"Not really, no more than any of us being homesick. Not until the last couple of weeks."

"Suicidal?" Chrys wanted to get in as many questions as she could before she lost her."

"I don't think so. She never talked about anything like that"

"What happened in the last few weeks that got her depressed?"

Louise shook her head. "I don't know. She didn't write about it in her journal? She was always writing in that thing. She asked me once who she'd report bullying to."

"Bullying? Chrys' Spidey sense tingled. "What kind of bullying? Who was bullying her?"

"I don't know." Louise stepped around Chrys. "I can't...I don't know."

"Bullshit." Chrys grabbed the woman's arm. "You do know. I can see it in your face. What did they do to her?" Chrys' eyes burned. She let go of the woman's arm as soon as she knew Louise wasn't going to walk away. Faint finger marks were visible on her forearm.

Louise stared at her. "I don't know! It was in the kitchen. I told her to talk to Karl or Chef Sam."

"But what did they do?"

The woman threw out her arms as she looked around. "I don't know."

Chrys half expected to see a man sitting on a park bench with eye holes cut out of a newspaper. Instead she saw the sun shining off the red roof of the clubhouse.

"She said something about a knife in her cutting board and maybe something in her drink. Read her journals. She had two of them."

"Two?"

"She finished one and started another." Louise checked the time and let out a frustrated sigh.

"Where are her notebooks?"

Louise shook her head. "Home with her parents I assume. Or maybe with her friend. When they cleaned out her side of the room they said they were sending it all."

"They? Who are they?"

Louise played with her fingernails. She sighed again. "Trent, Karl and Blaire. They came and cleaned out her stuff and did whatever with it. Look, I have to get going. I'm going to be late. Ask them what they did with her stuff."

They sent all of Tessa's belongings home, as far as Chrys knew. "When did you last see her write in her journal?"

Louise dropped her gaze to the pavement and turned her back as an SUV slowly drove past. Chrys looked at the charcoal car, but didn't see who was behind the tinted windows. When Louise turned back her face was almost white. "That morning. She had been writing in her new journal for a couple of weeks. I don't know where it is. I have to get to work."

Chrys had one more question to try. "What's Emerald?"

Louise didn't say a word. She sucked her bottom lip between her teeth and bit down hard enough to leave marks.

"Louise?"

"I work here." She walked backward a few steps toward the clubhouse. "I need this money. You don't know these people. If someone goes against them they go away just like Tessa."

"What's going on here, Louise? What did Tessa get into?" Chrys stared after the woman. She watched her hair bounce on her shoulders as the woman broke into a jog. This girl had things to tell Chrys that would be difficult to hear. One woman was dead, Chrys and Spencer had been shot at, and Hanni was in a hospital...Fontana was no paradise.

~ * ~

Chrys saw her brother sitting on the hood of Hanni's car before she crossed the highway. She had left Louise and run back to Birch Grove. Her arms swayed at her side as she marched to the car. Her eyes darted around. Nobody else was there. The RV camp was alive with activity.

"Get in," Chrys snapped as she unlocked the car with a push of a button.

For a moment, Spencer thought of protesting. His sister was only this serious on rare occasions and he knew to pay attention to it.

She had the car started and on the highway before either said another word. She drove south away from the lodge. Ahead they saw the eroded sandstone cliffs known as the Hoodoos, chalky-grey rock faces which appeared out of place standing in the valley with no other mountains or hills around.

When they turned off the highway just before the rock outcropping Spencer asked, "What's going on? Your text said to meet you outside, but didn't say we were going anywhere."

"I want to walk around and talk to you away from everyone else." Chrys stared at the road ahead.

Spencer snorted at a sign asking people to be on the lookout for cattle rustlers. He didn't realize that was a problem. It seemed more like a wild wild-west issue than a problem at a resort in the mountains.

Chrys pulled the car into a gravel parking area and stopped in front of a big sign that read "Welcome to the Hoodoos." A poster below that explained of how the cliffs were developed over millions of years of rain and flowing water against the soft rock. Another noted the Aboriginal belief that an enormous fish had been trying to swim between the mountains. It finally gave up and died, its rib cage becoming the Hoodoos. There was only one other car in the parking lot.

"So glad I dressed for a hike," Spencer commented. He wore black chef pants and a red and blue plaid shirt over a t shirt of one of the bands that played at The Alcrest.

Chrys glared at him with a look that shut him up.

The two of them started hiking the wide trail thick with the scent of sage. One side was forest and rock, the other opened to views of the valley.

Spencer waited for his sister to say something. He checked his phone for the time. "Remember I still have to get to work," He couldn't wait any longer.

"Fuck your fake job." Chrys looked behind them, then pulled her chestnut hair out of its knot and flipped it over her shoulders.

"I've been asked to work at the lodge today. I'll get some answers."

"I talked to Louise."

"When?"

"This morning. I waited outside your place until I saw her and then walked with her. I told her I was a reporter." She looked over her shoulder. Was that a car door shutting? Sounds seemed to come from everywhere and nowhere. "I think she's scared, Spence. She talked to me, but her body was shaking and her eyes were teary."

"What did she say about Tessa?"

Ahead a couple of women descended the hill with a bounce in their step as they tried to fight gravity. Conversations between Chrys and Spencer stopped until the women were gone. Chrys turned and watched the two women until they disappeared around a corner before starting to hike again.

"She said Tessa was being bullied and I think she might have Tessa's notebook. She didn't say that exactly. Caroline didn't have the latest one, so either Louise has it or someone did something with it."

"Let's go then." Spencer stopped.

Chrys grabbed his arm and pulled him to start walking again. "Not until after her shift and I don't know if she has it. She got pretty stressed when I asked her about Emerald. I don't know who she's afraid of, but she's scared of someone."

"I think you and Hanni should go home." Spencer couldn't enjoy the view of the widening river that curled around the mountain away from the lodge.

"What the hell are you talking about? I'm not fucking going home."

"Calm down, Chrys."

"I'm not going home, Spencer. I've been doing more work on this than you have..."

"Since when is this a competition, Chrys? This isn't about us."

"It's always about us." Chrys marched on ahead. She pushed through a couple of cedar branches and walked out into an open area near the top of the Hoodoos.

The trees gave way to white sandstone where very little could grow. It was like a beach on a mountain top. The ground took on a soft sandy texture from the tree-line on to the cliff edge. Any trees that rooted close to the edge looked dead and ancient with very few green at the ends of grey branches. The cliff stuck out in points like the fish in the Aboriginal myth. The closer one got to the edge the more they felt like some of the stone could crumble away. There were deep cracks in all directions. A hundred feet below, the highway twisted around the cliffs. It curved its way into the thick canopy of evergreens that covered the mountains and disappeared to the south. For a moment they forgot what they were arguing about as they stepped close to the edge. Only for a moment.

"Our whole life has been a damn competition, so what makes you think this is any different?"

Spencer leaned over to look between two "ribs" that reached out. It looked like a gentle slope at first then dropped off suddenly. One slip and you were gone. "I'm not competing with anyone. I want to find out if someone killed my friend and, if so, who did it. Either share with me what you have or don't."

"Shut up."

"I'm not going to..."

Chrys clapped her hand on her brother's mouth. His eyes opened wide. Their ears caught the faint sounds of voices. Someone was coming up the trail behind them and they were close.

"We have to go," Chrys said.

"It's just people coming up the trail."

Chrys grabbed hold of her brother's shirt and raised herself onto her toes to be face-to-face with him. "These guys own this place. They have the cops. Tessa isn't the first person they've killed. We have to move." Her eyes burned with an intensity.

"What?"

She led the way along the edge of the sage brush heading away from the main trail. They scrambled over the cuts in the sandstone. Their shoes slipped on loose rock. As he followed his fearless sister, Spencer tried not to look down at the edge and how close they were to falling to their deaths. She jumped one of the open crevasses and he had no choice but to follow. The treeline suddenly pushed back away from the cliff edge making the two of them jog out in the open. Both looked over their shoulders. The voices were louder.

"Where are they?"

"They have to be up here."

"Look around."

"Over here."

The men's voices echoed through the trees and off the stone. Chrys and Spencer couldn't tell how many men were back there or who they were. Spencer felt fear surge through his body. Everything seemed to tingle and his stomach ached. Excitement and adrenaline pounding through Chrys' limbs. She wasn't afraid.

"Hey, stop!"

Both of them skidded to a stop. Rocks rolled away from their feet. They turned around and looked back the way they had come. A man stood on the rib of rock; he was looking right at them. He wore the uniform of a Fontana security guard. There was crashing in the trees as other men broke free of the sage.

Spencer spun around and pushed his sister toward the woods. A gunshot cracked through the air beside them. Both flinched automatically, bending over as they crashed through branches. Chrys felt her arm get scratched. Her hands grabbed at branches and trees. She wished she was wearing a jacket. Spencer glanced back. The trees closed behind them so he couldn't see, but he could hear the men yelling. A branch slapped his face.

"Mother..."

Two more shots rang out. They heard a bullet thunk against a tree and saw splinters fly from another. Chrys' hand touched the spongy ground. Spencer grabbed her shirt and pulled her to the side. They exploded through thick trees, branches and needles tearing at their skin and clothes. In the woods there was no sign of the crumbling white rock. The disturbance caused a flock of birds to take flight. They heard the men crashing through the trees behind them.

The siblings broke from the woods into a meadow. Under other circumstances it would be picturesque with gently flowing grass and wildflowers. To them it was a death trap. Chrys took off through the woods running to the left of the direction they had been going. Spencer knew they were heading back toward the cliff edge.

A gun shot rang out and like geese in the air both Alcrests turned back into the woods as if synchronized. Chrys was ahead of Spencer, so he angled himself toward where she should be.

Chrys pushed through a thicket of trees. Her hands blocked her face from branches. She dug her heels into the earth.

Spencer didn't cover anything as he crashed through branches and trees. He turned sideways as he went through the last bush. His sister was there. She screamed something and reached out for him. Her fingers grasped his shirt. He saw the ground disappear from under him. He had come out between two ribs of sandstone.

Chrys' fingers slipped away and he dropped.

Spencer's feet hit the rock. Pebbles and stones careened down ahead of him. The slope was gentle, but the left rib came in quickly and he couldn't see what was beyond. There was an edge. The hill gave way to nothing.

Chrys dropped her body to the ground and reached out as if she might catch him. "Spence!"

Chapter 16

Chrys dove to the side and scrambled along the edge. She heard someone yell behind her. Her foot slipped over the side. She grabbed at trees and pulled herself along. They went right to the cliff edge. Roots had come free and dangled in the air. She looked down, but couldn't see her brother. She couldn't wait. She moved a few more steps along the edge then pulled herself into the woods. She dropped to her hands and knees crawling as fast as she could.

"Where are they?"

She dropped flat onto the ground. The damp grass soaked her clothes. She could hear the men breathing. She put her hand over her mouth to try and hide her own breathing.

"I know they came this way."

"Maybe they jumped over the edge."

There was a pause where Chrys imagined them leaning over the edge to look, probably seeing Spencer's broken body at the bottom.

"Nobody down there."

"The chick had a red shirt. How hard could she be to find?"

Chrys rolled rapidly under low hanging evergreen branches.

The same voice continued, "You go that way along the cliff and we'll go this way. Fire a shot if you see anything."

She saw two pairs of legs as the men crossed the edge of the cliff by hanging onto the trees as she had. Chrys tried to press herself further into the earth. She had put on the red top because it was going to be warm out and she wanted something that made her look nice. She was regretting it now. Even in the thicker woods it was a huge signal telling anyone where she was.

Chrys waited until she couldn't hear the men any more. She wasn't sure how much time had passed. Staying close to the ground she wiggled out of her blouse. Underneath she wore a bra (the website described the colour as cafe au lait - which was pretty close to her own skin colour) that had lacy flowers and leaves over the cups. Her cell phone stuck out of the left cup. She pushed her shirt back under the tree and scattered a handful of dead leaves over it, but that didn't help disguise the bright red.

As she crawled toward the sandstone cliff, her eyes scanned all directions. Her light caramel skin blended into the woods a lot better than the red blouse.

She looked over the edge where her brother had disappeared. She couldn't see him. "Spencer." She whispered and looked around wondering what the echo was like. "Spencer?"

A head appeared about ten feet below and then her brother stepped out. "Are they gone?"

"You asshole!"

"Shut up. Are you naked?" He had some blood on his arms.

Chrys tossed a rock down narrowly missing her brother. "It was too bright. How do we get you up?"

"I don't know if we can." When Spencer went over the edge he slid on the broken rock and landed on a ledge ten feet down. Right beside him one of the ribs had a hole eaten away by time and weather. He had climbed under it and waited. To the side the hill took a gentle slope downward with woods and actual solid area not far below. The hundred foot cliffs were back near the highway.

She looked back in the direction the two men had gone. Would they have heard her yell at her brother?

"Chrys, there are people trying to kill us. Get out of here. I can try getting down. I'll go straight for the highway."

"Hold on." She turned and scrambled beneath the trees again. The branches rubbed against her bare skin. She laid on the ground, wrapped one end of the blouse around her hand and let the rest of it hang down. "Grab onto this."

"Really?"

"What? Just grab hold and climb up."

Spencer pushed himself up on the rock and snatched the blouse. His other hand grabbed at the rock.

Dirt and rock exploded against Spencer's face as a bullet deflected against the cliff edge.

"Run!" Spencer dropped back down. He scrambled beneath the arch as sonic eruptions echoed around him. He flattened his body to the earth. Sandstone exploded on the cliff as bullets dug in. A scream escaped from his lips. He pushed his body into the cliff until rocks were biting into his flesh.

Chrys screamed at the first gunshot. She pushed away from the edge scurrying backward into the trees. She rolled over twigs and stones. Her body flinched every time a bullet rang out. These bullets sounded different. They weren't being fired at her. She had to do something, make a distraction and hopefully draw them away from her brother or take off for Hanni's car?

She jumped into a crouch. No gunshots came at her. It would be different with her blouse. Where was that? It didn't matter. She counted to three, spun and charged through the sage straight across the mountain top.

"They're shooting blind," Spencer said to himself. "They can't see me."

The gunshots stopped. A few more rocks tumbled down.

Spencer got himself into a crouch and flexed his knees. Something was coming. His fingers wrapped around the closest rock he could find. He saw feet, legs. A gun. He leapt forward as one of the men landed on his ledge. Spencer's hand came up, the rock in it connected with the man's forearm.

There was a scream. The gun dropped from his grasp and skidded in the dirt.

Spencer's body slammed against him and the man's back hit the hard rock. Their eyes met in wild surprise.

This man had fear in his. In Spencer's there was only survival.

Spencer twisted his body connecting his elbow with the other man's jaw. He heard bone and teeth grind together. He brought his knee up hard into soft flesh knocking all the fight out of the other man.

Spencer spun low, grabbed the handgun from the ground and ran through the arch and over the ledge.

His feet moved in the air. The moment he hit the slope he was running. White and grey stones avalanched down around him. There was no stopping here. He heard a yell and another gunshot. The slope turned so he was soon blocked from the top by a rib.

Spencer knew what would happen if he fell onto the rocky ground. He'd tumble down over the rocks tearing his body to pieces. Out of the corner of his eye he saw Chrys' red blouse clinging to a tiny shrub. He tried grabbing the cliff with his hands. He left chunks of flesh behind. Spencer felt awkward running down a cliff with a pistol in his hand. This was no movie. He wasn't going to jump in the air, spin, let off three shots taking out each of the bad guys, land on his feet and continue running. If anything he was going to fall down and shoot himself.

Spencer started jumping two feet at a time trying to dig his shoes into the earth. At the bottom he broke into a run into the forest.

~ * ~

Chrys dropped down to one knee and grabbed onto the closest tree. She couldn't control her breathing, so she tried to focus on letting air in and out. Her head spun and her chest burned. She had run straight up and over the hill, ignoring the screams and gunshots behind her, and stopped in sight of the parking lot. She had tree sap and twigs all over her body and in her hair. Her skin was covered with scratches.

A white Fontana security SUV was parked beside Hanni's car. She couldn't see anyone around. She had to get to the car and hope to find her brother before those guys got down here. She had to believe that Spencer got away.

Her body froze and she suddenly held her breath. A man stepped out from behind the SUV moving a cell phone in all directions. "Shit." Chrys wanted to shout out. It was Jonas.

Chrys looked down at her body. She was a dancer, a roller derby chick and she worked out almost every day. She looked good – even with sap and twigs all over her body. Her breasts might have been humble, but more than a handful was too much, and in this bra at first glance she'd look topless. She'd only seen Jonas once or twice at The Alcrest. Hopefully, his eyes would stop before they reached her face and he'd recognize her.

By keeping the SUV between them, she made her way from the trees without him seeing her. As she reached the back of the vehicle; she walked with the best model strut she could muster. Her hips swayed, she tossed her hair behind her head and pushed her breasts out.

Jonas heard her boots on the gravel first. As he turned his eyes caught the tight yoga pants and traveled up over her flat stomach and curves. When she stopped walking his eyes made it all the way up. They focused on her face. "I know you."

Like a soccer player kicking the ball all the way down the field, Chrys' foot shot upward between the man's legs.

She jammed her fingers at his eyes. She felt wet against her fingertips. He fell back and hit the security

217

vehicle. Before he hit the ground, Chrys was in the car. She turned the ignition and had the car away before Jonas moved. The tires spit rocks on his moaning body.

In her head she repeated a line from Karate Kid Three. "A man can't see, he can't fight."

~ * ~

"Drive!"

"I am driving." Chrys slammed her foot down on the gas pedal. Before she found Spencer, Chrys had been driving back and forth along the highway in front of the Hoodoos. She stopped once to carefully brush the broken glass from her body and put her jacket on. She had scratches all over her body. Every time she saw another vehicle coming toward her from the direction of the lodge she held her breath and waited for it to drive passed.

"We have to go back." Spencer had run straight toward the highway, never looking back, and sat in the edge of the trees waiting until he saw the car. His body ached. He was limping and held onto his side the whole time. The past and present had collided in a battle of pain through his entire body.

"Go back? Is that your blood on you? We can't go back."

He had red stains over his arm and on the side of his face. "None of it's mine. One of them dropped down from the top, so I hit him."

"Did you recognize the guy you hit?"

Spencer had the 9mm handgun stick inside his pants pocket. He had checked to make sure the safety was on first. "I don't know. I don't think so."

"Did any of them see you? You can't go to the lodge. They know who you are now. Jonas sure knows I'm here because I hit him."

"You hit Jonas?"

Chrys shrugged her shoulders. "He's probably walking funny and can't see too well."

"Turn around Chrys. I have to do this tonight." He stared at his sister until she made a U-turn. "Drop me off at the sub shop and I'll wash up."

"Spencer, you're being crazy."

"I have to end this, Chrys."

Chrys shook her head even though her brother wasn't looking at her. She might have caused all of this. They had been shot at again and this time they knew it was no accident. Those men were out to kill them. And yet her brother still had to go back?

"I'm going to be late for work." Spencer should have hitchhiked, but would probably be asked a lot of questions about his cuts and scrapes that he couldn't answer. It would have been so much easier than having to fight with Chrys. Spencer turned to his sister. "You should drop me off and go get Hanni. Get to the cops and tell them what happened."

She glared at him. "As far as we know these guys have the cops in their pockets. If we go to them we'll probably end up in the river or something."

"Is this a gangster movie now? This is real life, Chrys, and the closest cops are the RCMP. According to what we know these guys are drug dealers. According to what just happened to us they want to kill us and anyone in their path. Chances are they killed Tessa. A Mountie isn't going to do what a drug dealer tells him to do. Drop me off, so I can get to my job."

Chrys was tired, sweaty, covered in dirt and scratches and her expression at the moment probably made her look ugly. She had dealt with the same argument from her brother and their father. In a cook's life the job was paramount. "Screw you and your, *I'm a chef holier-than-thou god of cooking bullshit*. This isn't your job. You're pretending. These guys just tried to kill us. You go back and they will kill you."

"No they won't. Chef's not part of this." At least he sounded confident. "And I have to finish this."

"It's finished, Spence. Shoot at us once shame on them; shoot at us twice shame on us. Shoot at us a third time and we're fucked. We are out of here." She pulled the car to the side to make another U-turn.

Spencer grabbed the door handle. "You turn this car around and I'll jump out. I'll be fine, Chrys. You get to Hanni and I'll come tomorrow. This is my chance to get to the lodge and ask around. I can't let this go."

"Ask them not to shoot your face. I want you to have an open casket."

"Funny." He flexed his fingers around the handle of the handgun. It was as though he could feel its power pulse in his palm and through his thigh.

"I'm not leaving you then."

"Chrys, don't start."

She punched the steering wheel. "Fine. You keep the car though. I can always find a ride to Hanni." She had hitchhiked her way around Australia for one summer working on different farms and at restaurants. Getting a ride to Yanko was not going to be a problem. She was usually the one to do stupid things. Her brother had always been there to pull her back. She couldn't figure out which one of them was being stupid now.

"Chrys, I don't need the car, you do."

She glanced over and saw the seriousness in his eyes. She wasn't going to change his mind. "What about Louise? She could be in danger because of me."

"I'll make sure she's not. We'll all be fine, Chrys. I'll be fine."

For the first time she didn't know what to say. Every time she tried to speak her words got caught in her throat. "Fuck you then."

Chapter 17

It took Spencer longer than he thought to clean himself up in the bathroom at the sub shop. His shirt was torn. His chef pants were stained with white sandstone dust. There were spare clothes at Northview. As he walked down the road, the handgun was wrapped in his plaid shirt with his left hand tight around the grip. If anyone started shooting at him he was prepared to ruin a perfectly good shirt, even though he had never shot a handgun before. Rifles, yes when he went hunting with dad as a teenager, but not a 9mm pistol. The weight was surprising. In movies they whipped them around without a care in the world; however, his arm was already getting tired.

Chrys and Hanni were safe, at least he knew that part. He'd worry about Louise when he could. This was going to be his one chance to find out who killed Tessa. His sister was going to get the cops in there one way or another, so his time to question people was limited.

He marched into his kitchen at Northview Golf Course. Amam stared at him from behind the line as he was cooking, but didn't say a word. Spencer felt powerful. He had a gun hidden in his hand and could quite possibly be going to his death, so what did he have to lose. "Where's Kevin?"

"He left already," Bobbi said as she put clean plates back beside the pass.

"Stuart?"

"Organizing the cooler."

De to the adrenaline flowing through his body, Spencer was breathing rapidly. "Okay. I have to go work at the lodge, so you and he are closing." He said nothing else, walked into the washroom, closed and locked the door.

He unwrapped his hand and placed the gun next to the sink. It made a tick and thunk on the ceramic. On the side it said it was a 9mm made by Smith and Wesson. In the mirror he saw a man in a whirlpool of emotion. He splashed his face with cold water. There were scrapes on the right side of his face. His arms were scratched and bloodied from when he fell down the cliff. He lifted cold water into his blond hair slicking it back. Water dripped down the back of his neck.

"Spencer?" Bobbi's voice came through the bathroom door. "Chef Sam is here for you."

He stared into his eyes through the mirror. "I'll be right there." He tore off some brown paper towel from the dispenser, dried off his face and ran it back over his hair. Chef pants were not made to hold a gun in the waistband. After putting on a new pair, he tried sticking it in the back and it slipped down. Spencer re-wrapped it in his plaid shirt and exited the room.

Spencer unrolled his knife roll and rolled it back up with the shirt and gun inside before he slung it over his shoulder and snatched his chef coat from the hanger. The way Bobbi looked at him she appeared to be afraid. He wondered if it had to do more with working with Amam than anything else. Perhaps she knew more than he thought she did about everything. Perhaps word of what happened had already spread through the lodge - or it was all in Spencer's head? Any one of the people he had met since coming to Fontana could have been involved in Tessa's death. It was like going through a maze blindfolded and with your hands tied behind your back. Everyone was a suspect, even the kitchen staff.

"You ready to go?" Chef Sam put his phone in his pocket. "We're pretty busy." He sat on an ATV outside the back door. He saw the look on Spencer's face and added, "This is faster through the back trail than the truck on the road. I only have one helmet though."

As the engine fired up the sound was so familiar. Spencer had heard it in the mountains. This could have been the very same ATV that chased them over a cliff. Chef Sam could have been the man who shot Chrys. He could have been Tessa's killer.

Spencer climbed on and grasped the rear mounting bars as the quad took off. Tufts of grass marked where the old trailers had been and cracked dirt and cut pipes completed the scene. They took a back trail worn down by quads and staff walking back and forth from Birch Grove to the main lodge. It would have been the same path Tessa took every day. There were no lights. On her last night she probably walked down this path afraid of what was behind her. Someone could have been lying in wait.

"Are you ready?" Chef had taken his helmet off, his red hair emblazoned under the sun.

"Yeah, I guess. Say, can anyone use the ATV?"

"Management mostly, but if anyone asked it would probably be okay. You just have to sign out the keys at the front desk. I'm going to sign these back in and I'll take you to the kitchen. What happened to your face by the way?"

"I fell walking up the hill." Spencer watched the keys dangling from his boss's fingers. Sam could have been the one in the mountains.

He followed Chef Sam inside and watched as he slipped behind the reception desk. The keys went onto a hook on the side wall. He wrote the time on a clipboard taken from a corner drawer. Clipped beneath the page he signed was a stack of ruffled

226

pages. If somebody had the quad the other day their name would be on that list.

Spencer looked to the right and saw Blaire behind the desk staring at him. She didn't have the friendly glow she'd had on his first day. A smile appeared on her face as the two of them walked away, but there was no emotion behind it.

The moment the door to the kitchen opened, Spencer heard the sounds he knew so well. At Northview they weren't busy, so there was no excitement. He missed having The Alcrest full on a Saturday night: running out of prepped ingredients two thirds through the rush, yelling at servers to get their shit together and the delicate dance of his small brigade between the hot equipment and the counter.

He loved the sounds. Thuck, thuck, thuck, thuck, thuck...thuck, thuck, thuck - someone was good with a knife. The noise of the exhaust fans forced everyone to raise their voices. A dust and grease covered ghetto blaster played music from someone's iPod. The speakers were attached by a wire that had electrical tape on one end and was strategically draped over old bread baskets and thumb tacks in the wall to counteract loose wires. A food processor spun. The order machine spit out a printed chit. The dishwasher slammed down and roared to life. Even The Alcrest wasn't like this. This was more like the high end restaurants he had worked in after culinary school.

"Spencer," Chef Sam grabbed his attention, "You're going to be on prep. I know it's not sous chef work, but we need it done fast and right. We're really behind."

"Why are you behind so much?" Spencer let his eyes travel over all of faces trying to see if he recognized anyone who may have chased them.

"Banquets and staff on other projects. Plus someone got hurt hiking today."

Hurt hiking or hurt chasing the Alcrests off a cliff, Spencer mused to himself.

"Karl come here. I'm going to give you to Karl and you can go to it."

Karl nodded at the new man. "So you're my bitch, eh?" His broken tooth showed when he smiled. He had two new scratches on his stubbled cheek that weren't there the last time they met.

"Guess so." *Could the scratches be from running through the woods?* As Spencer looked around the room he felt like everyone was looking at him. Each person he focused on looked back at him. None smiled. A couple nodded. All of them could be involved with Emerald. Considering what happened two months ago in the back kitchen of a nightclub in Middleton he wasn't sure how much trouble he was in. He had taken Advil earlier, but the phantom pain he was feeling was still there.

"You've got some nasty cuts there," Karl said with a nod.

"You too."

"Yeah," Karl dragged the word out. Both men stared at each other for a long moment before the sous chef's lips curled back from his teeth in a questionable smirk.

"You can work here. Recipes are in a blue binder over there. Start with getting the ribs going and then go down the list. Prep list is on the whiteboard."

Spencer gave him a nod. In fifteen minutes he had a rondo on the back stovetop with racks of pork ribs, lime halves, bay leaves, spices inside and watered down apple juice inside. As soon as it started boiling he wrapped the top in foil and got the whole thing in the oven. The staff initialed each recipe after the first time they made something. He found Tessa's initials in the bottom right corner of the rib recipe.

The table where Spencer worked was around the corner from the main action and forced him to have his back to everything. He chewed on his bottom lip. Sweat formed on his temples. Every couple of minutes he glanced over his shoulder because he felt like someone was there, but no one was.

The topic of the girl who killed herself came up whenever he went to "ask someone a question." A prep cook and two of the dishwashers were hired after she died or just before and didn't really have a chance to talk to her. Payton, the one with the good knife skills, said Tessa got extremely quiet shortly before her death. She never said what was going on and Payton never asked. He saw the server Chrys had told him about (the one who'd given her information), but didn't get to talk to her. After talking to one cook, "Hey, I've been curious about what went down with that chick who killed herself," he got an, "I don't know anything," and watched him run to Karl and whisper in his ear. Karl only nodded.

"Spencer," Karl was suddenly beside him, sweat caked on his face. There was a perspiration stain along the bottom of his cap. "How's it going? What do you think so far?"

Spencer laid his knife down on the board, his fingers still wrapped around the handle. "You have a good crew." Aquamarine eyes stared into black ones.

Karl never let his gaze falter. "You should take a break. Get something to eat."

Spencer's fingers relaxed. "I will." He slipped from his apron and left the kitchen looking back over his shoulder as he walked. Karl stayed at the prep station leaning back against the table and watching him.

Spencer walked past the open door to the staff room. He hadn't seen Chef Sam since being left in the lion's den and didn't know where he was. He had been waiting to get out of the kitchen. Spencer walked swiftly down the hallway toward the front door to the lodge. With a glance over his shoulder he rounded the front reception desk.

"Can I help you?" Blaire blasted. "You can't come back here." Two customers were waiting for her attention.

Spencer ignored her and took the ATV clipboard from the wall.

"You can ask for that, you know. You have to go through proper channels." She ignored the customer checking in and came to Spencer. Her fingers grasped the top of the clipboard only to have it pulled away by him.

Spencer looked up with a flat grin. He said, "Sorry," handed her the board and headed back toward the kitchen. He'd seen what he needed to. He knew who had signed out the ATV the day he and Chrys were up in the mountains.

As he stepped into the staff dining room he heard his name called. Chef Sam sat at a table in the corner farthest from the food. Spencer felt eyes on him again. He got a small plate of rigatoni and meat sauce and a bottle of water before making his way to the chef. He couldn't tell who was looking at him but he didn't like the feeling. It was the ominous feeling of being watched that horror movies always tried to make you feel. He remembered a song from the 80's about private eyes watching you.

As he pulled out the chair across from the chef he recognized the knife roll sitting on the table. His plaid shirt was draped over it. Again his back was to everyone. "That's mine."

Chef Sam rested his hand on the knife roll. "Karl gave it to me. He said we didn't need you any more today." His hand went dropped from the roll as he flashed a skeleton smile.

"Busy place, eh?" Spencer pushed his food around. Where was the gun? Who was the bad guy?

"That it is." Chef Sam pushed away from the table. He had only eaten half of his food. "I have to get back to paperwork. One of the guys said he saw you at the Hoodoos."

Spencer's eyes flicked around. He said, "Wasn't me," before filling his mouth with rigatoni and sauce.

Chef Sam glanced around the room before staring at Spencer. "In case you do, be careful. We don't want to be out another cook. And be careful when you're walking to and from your shifts."

The man's voice was very calm. There was no menace at all. Spencer couldn't decide if his life had just been threatened. However, he'd lost all interest in food.

Chapter 18

In one move Chrys jumped from sitting on the floor to crouching like a cat ready to pounce. She was on the balls of her feet with fingertips barely touching the carpet for balance. She heard voices outside the door. She was all set to back up into the closet if a key was inserted into the lock.

After looking around the room Chrys settled by the door and made her phone calls. She had to see if she could get them any help. It was a lot later than she had hoped when she heard the voices.

"So in the Philadelphia Experiment," came a voice through the door to the hallway, "they were playing with time travel, right. When this ship reappeared some of the men, the sailors were, like, melted into the ship."

Chrys knew that voice; it was Jonas.

She didn't like lying to her brother, but sometimes that was a lot easier than trying to convince him to see things her way. After they split, she did head toward Yanko but turned around after half-an-hour and headed back to Fontana.

The souvenir shop had a bit of everything. At least half the their items had to do with Fontana and/or the hot springs while the other half had to do with country and/or mountain living. There was a nice collection of lamps, picture frames and a coat rack made of horseshoes. She purchased a tank-top with a roaring bear on it before stopping to look through a rack of writing journals. Her fingers stopped at one with a waterfall pictured on the front cover.

She knew that book.

Chrys put the shirt on in the car, tied her hair back and drove to Birch Grove. She parked the car inside the RV park. A little flirtation and a story about surprising her boyfriend and she had a family watching the car with no driver's window.

She waited a while hoping most of the morning workers would be back in their rooms asleep. As she approached the side door to the hotel building it opened and she froze. She thought for a second what she would do if Jonas walked out. She curled her fingers into fists. One knee bent – ready to strike. The stranger smiled at her and held the door.

The next step was tricky. When she got home she was going to have to thank Bert who owned the locksmith shop down the street from their restaurant. He had been her dad's best friend and gave her work when she needed extra cash. As Louise's door opened she was grateful Bert had showed her how to pick locks. Two minutes though meant she was out of practice. She had been waiting ever since.

"So that's why I believe in time travel and that the government is covering it up. Nobody really wrote about it and there were no movies about it until then, you know." Jonas was still crazy.

"I'll look it up." That was a woman's voice. She sounded happy and encouraging.

"You should. You should look it up. There are videos on YouTube and there's a movie, an actual movie, called The Philadelphia Project. You should check those out and then we could talk about it."

When he worked at The Alcrest Jonas barked like a seal and slapped his hands in front of him. He liked to do everything his way and didn't like to listen. He was a strange one. Maybe The Pass at Fontana was the perfect place for him. Chrys had to get Spencer out of there and back to his own cooking. She still wasn't sure why Tessa ended up there

"I will. I'll look it up." The woman was trying to get away from him.

A key slipped into the lock. Chrys actually came close to saying, "shit," out loud. She backed into the closet, still crouched down, and scooted back away from the opening. She pushed the sliding door to where it had been when she came in. She should be well hidden.

The front door opened. Louise said goodbye to Jonas and shut the door. Chrys heard the click of the bolt lock. She had to bide her time and wait. If she made her move the woman could warn someone. The shower was turned on. Chrys waited until she was out of the shower.

It had taken longer than she thought it would to get into Louise's room. She had to stop a couple of times when another woman came down the hallway and Chrys pretended to be a new employee. When she got into the room she took a quick look around to see if she could find Tessa's journal. There were a few books on the dresser. One had a red cover with a hand digging in dirt and looked like a good read, but it wasn't what she was looking for. The more she thought about it the more she wondered if the journal even existed or if it was here. This woman could have lied.

She also could have been the reason the two Alcrests were almost killed.

The shower turned off. She heard Louise using an electric razor and do whatever else her post-shower ritual involved. Then the television turned on.

Chrys stood. She slid the closet door open. "Did you send Tessa's journal..."

"Oh my God!"

"...or was that just bullshit?"

Louise stumbled back. Her leg hit the bed and she fell into a sitting position. She had an orange towel wrapped tightly around her body, a yellow one on her head. At first she didn't seem to recognize the woman who had interviewed her this morning. The moment she did a darkness seemed to fall over her expression.

Chrys was well aware of the room. There were two beds with two dressers along the opposite wall. The window was behind Louise, with blinds closed, and it was too small for anyone to get through. The only way for Louise to get out of this situation would be through the door behind Chrys. She wasn't getting out of this. Answers needed to be found.

"Well?"

"How did you get in here?"

"Where's the journal?" Chrys' hands were at her side, fists balled tight enough that she could feel her trimmed nails digging into her palm.

Louise's mouth was wide open. Her eyes darted around as she looked for an answer. "This is my room. You can't just …"

"After talking to you this morning three or four men chased me and my brother through the woods. They shot at us. They tried to kill us. They shot me.

"Brother?"

Shit! "Either you called someone and turned us in or it was a great coincidence. Look at me. I didn't get these scratches hanging out in your closet." She had used the bathroom at the grocery store to clean herself up as best she could. She had a few scratches on both arms and one on her neck she hadn't known about. There was colourful bruising all around the bandaged gun graze.

"Who are you? Who's your brother?" Louise quickly got to her feet. "I don't have to take this."

As she took a step forward, Chrys grabbed her shoulders and pushed her. The woman fell back onto the bed where her clothes had been tossed before the shower, then she lunged forward.

Chrys twisted her body. Her hand flew out. The palm connected with the side of Louise's face and a loud smack engulfed the room. Chrys' hand burned.

Louise spun to the side. She reached out toward the wall and the bed. When she turned back she was on her knees holding the orange towel. The yellow one on her head had fallen off letting wet hair drape down over her eyes. Tears streamed over the red mark where Chrys' hand had slapped her.

"Are you done?" Chrys said. She was trying to play it cool, but her hand was throbbing. Her breath came fast. She felt nervous. She readied herself in case the woman made another move toward her. She didn't know if her legs could take it; she didn't know if any part of her could take it. In the last few seconds the tables had turned. She pushed that thought aside and realized her hand was starting to swell. "My brother was a friend of Tessa's and we want to find out the truth. She wouldn't have killed herself."

Louise kept her hand on her face. She glared up and said, "Maybe you didn't know her as well as you think. She was depressed and lonely. She had stopped talking to everyone. She'd come back here, write in her journal, and just go to bed. I tried to get her to go to the bar or to staff outings, but she'd say she didn't want to deal with anyone."

Chrys took a step forward and Louise flinched. "Where's the journal?"

"Do you even know who you're dealing with? They won't let you go." Louise's eyes were blazing. "I told you, they took everything and said they were sending it home. Go hit them."

The longer Chrys was in this place the more unsafe she felt. What if someone did see her or told someone about the new girl fumbling around the rooms? She wasn't safe. Spencer wasn't safe. She had no idea what was next, but she had to get out of here. "You told them about me didn't you? You're the reason we were almost killed."

Louise ran one hand through her hair while keeping the other on her towel, lifting the wet mess from her face and shoulders. "Bradshaw saw you with me. He's the one who drove past us. What was I supposed to do?" She rose to her feet and walked around the bed. "He picked me up and asked who you were. I said you were a reporter asking about Tessa. I don't know what happened next. I have two kids, you know. They're with my parents, but I pay for everything."

He probably followed Chrys after she got her brother, found out where they were going and had his men go after them. "You pay for your kids with the money you make by selling drugs. I know what goes on here. Who's Bradshaw?"

Louise sat down on the bed, her back to Chrys, and turned on the lamp which sat on a table between the two beds. "He owns Fontana; he owns everything. He has a crew cooking Emerald up at the ski lodge and it gets distributed through us. Everyone who works here and the cops are all under his thumb." Her eyes darted over her shoulder. They were hazel and at the moment wide and full of emotion. When she spoke about this Bradshaw there was a sense of fear. "He knows about you. He knew about you before I told him." She turned away.

"If I leave you now, are you going to tell him about me this time? Are you going to turn me in?" Chrys' body tingled. She didn't know if it was fear or excitement. It was adrenaline taking hold of her body.

Louise continued to sob. "I have my kids. You don't know what he'll do." Her body shook.

Chrys was afraid to move. This resort was a large factory for this drug known as Emerald. People came up here from the big cities to play a little golf and get their fix. The booze girls carried all the risk. How much of this did Tessa see?

"What are you doing?" In three steps Chrys was across the room. She pulled the other woman's

240

shoulder back. "A cellphone? Who were you texting? Bradshaw?"

"No." Louise tried getting up, but was pushed back.

Chrys ran to the door and threw it open. She heard someone running on the stairs. She turned and took off.

A man's voice yelled out behind her.

She suddenly felt fine. Her legs pounded. She hit the panic bar on the door at the end of the hallway. In the falling daylight she took a hard left, and got around the building. A few of the permanent RV campers had fences around their areas. Chrys focused her eyes on a three foot fence behind Birch Grove.

Someone else hit the door.

Chrys took to the air. Her legs curled over the top of the fence. As she landed she continued to run. She zigzagged around the campers away from where she left the car. Clouds had collected above the valley. The sound of thunder rolled between the mountains. She had to get to her brother.

Chapter 19

"It was a dark and stormy night." Spencer couldn't get that line out of his head. Lightning flashed in the clouds. With the flashlight on his pone, he searched ahead, carefully grabbing trees to steady himself as he walked down the Cliffside trail. He thought how no story that started with that classic line ended well for the guy alone in the woods.

Northview wasn't closed yet, so all he had to do was get there. The storm clouds had brought a swift end to the daylight.

The path was well worn. Staff came up and down here several times a day. Tessa had been on this very path. On her last night, she may have grabbed the same trees.

Spencer looked behind him. He could still see light from the windows of the main lodge. There were no other shadows. Of course someone could have driven down below and could be waiting for him.

The old staff trailers were gone, but the maintenance sheds and that old barn were still there. There were probably all kinds of rafters in those from which to hang someone.

His flashlight turned off. The cliff-side was suddenly dark. Thunder rolled. He heard leaves and shuffling. Human, animal or wind? Spencer pushed a button on his phone bringing the screen to life and then he hit the flashlight app. The forest was lit up again, but he still didn't feel good. His arms tingled. His breathing was rapid.

He took another step and his kitchen clog slipped out from under him. He grabbed at a tree. Somewhere behind him was at least one man with a gun and he couldn't make it down this stupid hill.

~ * ~

Chrys leaned forward, carefully looking around the back corner of a camper. Someone had followed her into the campground, but she had lost them long ago. She wasn't even sure how many had been after her. She was merely going by the sounds she heard behind her.

The campground was settled with people ready for the storm. A few families still sat around fires in their designated sites. Some had patio lanterns strung up. The wind was making things swing and sway. A Calgary Flames flag had already twisted itself tight around a pole. A lawn chair was on its side. A mother yelled for her kids to come in. A man carried an armload of firewood was with an arm load. Someone else walked a wiener dog on a leash. She was probably the only person who looked out of place here.

"Hey, you're back."

Chrys' back muscles tensed.

"Did I startle you?" The middle aged man Chrys had left her car with stepped down from his camper with a freshly opened beer bottle in his hand.

Chrys took a quick look in all directions. "No. I was just…I didn't expect you."

"Expecting someone else?"

"Something like that." Chrys tried to smile.

Without putting his bottle down, he opened the top of a barbeque and started flipping burgers. "I hope you don't mind; I taped some plastic over your driver's window." A thin layer of clear plastic was stuck over the open hole with silver duct tape. "Tricky to see out, but it should get you to Yanko where you can get it fixed."

"Thank you." Chrys smiled with full lips, however her dark eyes darted around. There was a time that she climbed into a vehicle and had an earring torn off her earlobe. She scoped out the back seat before opening the door.

"A guy asked about the car." The man closed the barbeque as the rain started to fall. "I told him it was mine and to go fuck himself."

Chrys crossed over to the man and pressed her lips to his check. As she drove out of the RV-park she saw Jonas watching by the doorway to Birch Grove. If ever there was a time to leave this place, this was it.

~ * ~

Spencer stopped. In front of him was the paved road leading to the model home. He still had to a few meters before he would pass the maintenance sheds. There were lamps along the road, so he knew no one was there. But now he had to step out into the light. He would be a cozy target. The man with the rifle could be up the hill or down by the dark corner of the maintenance shed waiting with one eye at the end of a scope. Was it Chef Sam, Karl or someone else?

He hated feeling afraid. This was all Chrys' fault. Before the happenings at the cistern the only thing that scared Spencer of was not being able to pay his bills. Now, after serial killers and being tortured, he was afraid of everything. He had been sitting in a ditch for ten minutes because he was terrified to go out onto the bright road.

He took a deep breath and ran out into the light.

~ * ~

The moment Chrys pulled away from Birch Grove she looked at the rear-view mirror. Nobody was following her. She didn't know if anyone saw her leave. She was going to pick up her brother, find Hanni and get the fuck out of the mountains.

She turned off of the highway and checked again. No cars were behind her.

Her skin was crawling. People were out there watching them, following them, chasing them and the Alcrests didn't know who those people were.

As Chrys turned left at the corner where she usually waited for Spencer a garage door opened. Light beamed out. Headlights turned on behind her. Were they waiting or was it coincidence? She pushed the gas pedal.

At the Northview parking lot she turned in and her he headlights fell on the old barn. There were three cars in the lot. All were probably staff. She pulled the car to the back door.

"Chrys!"

Her boot slipped on the ground as she was halfway out of the car. A dark shadow stepped from around the corner. Again she looked behind her. The other car had stopped where the parking lot met the road. What the hell was this?

"Chrys," the shadow called again.

"Spencer? What the hell?"

He came around to her side of the car. He looked better than the last time they'd seen each other. His eyes were wide and he kept looking over his shoulder.

"We have to get out of here." She turned and stared at the headlights of the other car. It wasn't moving.

Spencer unsuccessfully wiped the rain from his face. "Karl signed the ATV out the day we went hiking. I think Chef Sam's in on it too."

"Everyone's in on it, Spence. We have to get Hanni. We have to go now." Chrys shoved her brother's arm and he didn't fight her. In a few seconds they were both in the car. As she turned it around she expected the other vehicle to do something. She recalled what Louise had said about how they wouldn't let them go. She didn't know what was going to happen.

She didn't tell her brother who she thought was in the SUV. She saw the man's shape as they got close, but Spencer became quiet as though he already knew. Everything seemed to slow down. Chrys couldn't see through the other windshield. All she saw was an orange glow as the driver sucked on a cigarette or cigar. Her eyes stayed on the vehicle, even after it disappeared behind her plastic covered window.

The SUV didn't move.

They were halfway to the corner before Chrys saw its taillights flash in her rear-view mirror. It might not have been Bradshaw.

~ * ~

"Here are your discharge papers, Honey."

Hanni didn't like the way the nurse said her name. "It's about time. I can get dressed, right?" She threw the hospital bedsheets off and quickly sat up. She wore a lime green gown – the kind that tied in the back.

"Of course you can." The nurse was trying to be as calm as she could with her patient. She turned to leave.

"Have you seen Chrys?"

"Your friend?"

Hanni's eyes rolled as she crossed the room to where her clothes were folded on a chair. "Sure." She wouldn't call her that.

"She hasn't been here all day."

"Great." Hanni dropped the gown before the nurse pulled the curtain and left.

She looked fine. Hanni's skin was always on the paler spectrum anyway. She didn't have make-up, so she felt plain. Her head hurt. There was a pounding behind her eyes that was far worse than the thunder outside. She was going to have to stick with her regular drug of choice from now on. The other stuff was fun sometimes, however being slammed on her ass – not so much.

The night Chrys and Spencer didn't come back from their hike Hanni decided to say, "Screw it," and walk down to the bar. In ultra-tight skinny jeans and legs up to her neck she didn't have to walk far. Two drinks in and Kevin arrived. One more drink and he brought out a baggy with small green crystals in it. They smoked the first one in the car and it shot her to the moon. It was more intense than the powder she put up her nose. All of her muscles felt like they lifted from her bones. The second hit sent her on a trip like no other. It was wild enough that Hanni didn't know how she got back to her room. She didn't know if anything happened with her and Kevin. All she knew next was that Chrys and Spencer had her in the cold shower.

Thinking about the experience on her hospital bed made her tingle. Perhaps she would do it again someday.

"Hello?" A man's voice called out.

Hanni pushed the curtain aside. Chrys had left her a clean pair of jeans and a sweater that she was just pulling down. "Yeah?"

The man was tall and thin. He had stubble on his cheeks. "Hi, Spencer asked me to give you a ride." When he smiled there was a broken tooth. "I'm Karl." He had that ruggedly handsome aura that people talked about.

"Spencer sent you?" Hanni pushed the sweater sleeves up to her elbows. Her blue eyes looked the man up and down. It didn't make sense. Spencer was undercover. He wouldn't send some stranger to get her. She knew her boss and knew how he thought. "Where is he?"

"Back at Fontana. He wanted me to give you a ride." Karl put one hand in a jacket pocket.

Hanni felt sweat on her temple. This was all wrong. "I…I think I'll wait here."

Karl glared across at her. His smile vanished. "I don't think so."

"Hanni!" Spencer stepped through the door. He slid across the room and placed a hand on the blond woman's arm. He stared at the other sous chef. "Shouldn't you be working, Karl?" He pulled on Hanni's arm.

Karl's arm flexed. "Shouldn't you?"

Spencer and Hanni took a step toward the door. "Does Chef know you're here?"

"He's not the one paying the bills."

"Is Bradshaw?"

"You're in over your head."

"Spencer," Chrys was suddenly in the doorway of the small hospital room, "I called Constable Wright."

Spencer watched the other cook's arm relax and the intense stare slip away. "Karl, can you tell Chef Sam I quit?" He pulled Hanni toward the door. As they got close to it he pushed her through first.

"I'll see you at the Alcrest." Karl wasn't smiling any more. He stared at Spencer in a way that said he knew everything.

One more look passed between the two men before Spencer left the room. He quickly followed the two women who were well on their way toward the exit at the far end. As he caught up to them he glanced back over his shoulder. The other sous chef watched them from outside the room. Spencer put his lips close to his sister's ear. "What did Wright say?"

"I haven't called him yet." Chrys and Hanni ran through the rain.

Chapter 20

Chrys rang the doorbell and stepped back. She didn't feel good. Her upper arm burned beneath a sterile bandage and wrap. The doctor said she was going to have a scar. Just add that to all the others, she thought. What she really didn't like was the feeling that sticking your neck out for people wasn't worth it.

Spencer leaned back against the railing as his eyes surveyed the yard. He still couldn't shake the feeling that people were watching him. After getting Hanni they had driven all night to Middleton, then spent almost a whole day talking to the police. Some of the revelations were shocking. After a well-needed sleep his sister dragged him here. He wanted to get to the kitchen and avoid this moment all together. He wanted to feel safe.

As the door opened they heard a woman gasp, "What happened to you two?"

"It looks worse than it is." Chrys flashed a smile she hoped was calming. Both Alcrests had cuts and scrapes on their faces and arms. They would heal. "Can we come in?"

Caroline led the way into her living room. She quickly turned off the television, getting rid of the cartoons, and motioned for them to sit down. "I just took my son upstairs. He's not feeling will."

"I'm sorry. We won't stay long. We just wanted to tell you what happened." Spencer sat on the corner of the couch with his sister beside him.

Caroline sat in a lounge chair. The living room was clean, cleaner than you'd expect with a little kid in the house. Anything expensive was places above a certain height.

"So, I went to Fontana." Spencer watched her wring her hands together. This was not a good moment for anyone.

"And I followed," Chrys added. She wasn't here for this. There was still another path to go down. "Would you mind if I got a drink of water?"

"I only have tap water." Caroline pushed herself forward.

Chrys was on her feet in a second. "Don't worry, I can get it. You two talk." She bounced toward the kitchen where she had sat with their host before. Her brother went on talking about what had happened at The Pass at Fontana.

She turned on the cold water in the kitchen sink. The kitchen was as clean as the rest of the house. Dishes were all put away and there were no crumbs anywhere. A vase of flowers stood in the center of the kitchen table. She leaned around the flowers and saw the only thing out of place, a set of Lego blocks. The construction had changed a little. The base had not. Chrys knew the book she had seen in the souvenir shop was familiar. The same picture of a waterfall was there underneath the Lego house. She carefully removed the toy blocks before picking up the book. On the first page she saw Tessa Knelman's name. She almost felt sorry for hitting Louise; no she didn't.

"Anyone else want water? It's nice and cold." She hadn't touched it yet. Her eyes were on the hand-written words on the pages of Tessa's last journal.

Two, "no thank you's" came from the living room.

Spencer watched Caroline's face as he spoke. She followed every word. Her fingers were turning red from her squeezing them.

"So, that was when we left. We still can't say with one hundred percent certainty who all played a part in this and who might have killed Tessa. I'm pretty sure Karl was the one who shot at us." When he told that story he left out that his sister got hit with the bullet. "Constable Wright, our friend in the Middleton police, found out yesterday that Karl was killed in a car accident on his way back from Yanko to Fontana."

Caroline wiped tears from her cheeks. "That's a bit convenient."

"That's what I thought. The police are involved now and are going to move in on the drug operation. I think it's safe to say Tessa's killer is gone." Spencer didn't know what he believed.

"I'm tired. I'm so, so tired." Chrys' voice was so soft it was barely audible.

Spencer looked up at his sister standing just inside the living room. Caroline turned and rose to her feet when she saw what the Aboriginal woman was holding.

Chrys continued reading from the journal. "I don't know any more if this job is for me. I'm just so tired. I've trained so long at this career and can't find my way. I'm just not good enough. It will be over soon. I hope Mom and Dad and Caroline can forgive me. I just want the pain to be over. I just want to rest." She closed the book and held it to her chest. A tear made its way down her cheek.

"What are you doing with that?"

"What have you been doing with it this whole time, Caroline?" Chrys stepped back as the other woman stepped forward. "You must have read this."

"It doesn't prove anything."

"I got shot in the arm. We both almost died. Our friend was almost killed and you knew all of this." She held up the journal.

Caroline snatched it from her hand. She squeezed it tightly with both hands until her knuckles were white. She looked at the floor. She was a woman in turmoil. Her brain and heart were in a constant battle. "Tessa would never have done anything like that." Her voice was so firm in its conviction that Chrys thought maybe she read it wrong. "I want you two to leave."

Spencer glared at his sister. Since leaving Yanko they had barely spoken. They obviously had different ideas about what had happened to his friend. When he first travelled to Fontana he wasn't sure. After working in the lodge kitchen and feeling uncomfortable, he concluded that Tessa had been murdered. Now? He knew the job of being a chef could often take people to dark places. Drugs, alcohol, late hours…it all added up; she wouldn't have been the first cook to kill herself. "Caroline, you have to think about this."

"Spencer, you knew her. She wasn't like that." She marched to the front door and held it open. "Thank you for what you did. But I'll be hiring a professional to finish the job and find out who killed Tessa."

~ * ~

"This is bullshit." Chrys paced around the room.

"Anything is possible, Chrys. If Caroline wants to keep looking into Tessa's death that's up to her."

257

Deep down he knew what happened to his friend and though the tension around the lodge might have pushed things over the edge, he was certain nobody there had anything to do with it.

"Not that, you ass. You bitch about me getting a tiny tattoo and you go and get another one." Her dark eyes looked to the tattoo artist. "That is what is bullshit."

"Your tattoo's not tiny." Spencer grimaced as the needle touched his skin. He decided to get Tessa's feather tattoo on his calf. He also wanted to check out Sloane.

"It's not big either. And it's pretty."

"You two are great. You have a great friendship." Sloane's Aussie accent was music to Chrys' ears. Even Spencer had to admit it was intoxicating. She was a lovely-looking woman, far more *altered* than anyone either of them had ever been involved with, but that's what added to her appeal.

Chrys caught Sloane looking at her. She now knew what swooning felt like. "Why don't you get another tattoo?" She turned her eyes to the tattoo drawings on the walls.

Spencer rolled his eyes. There comes a time in every brother and sister relationship when sometimes you have to embarrass the other one just to shut them up. He turned to Sloane and said, "She has the hots for you."

"Spencer!" Chrys' eyes met the woman's and she turned away to focus on the drawings again. Her brother was such an ass. Her face was instantly hot.

"It's about time she admitted it." Sloane said with her head down concentrating on the art work. She bit her lip. "I can't wait forever to be asked out."

When Chrys turned back her face was all flushed and her knees felt wobbly. Spencer turned to look at her. Her brother was an ass. He was also her hero. "You know what I'm thinking? A tattoo every time we solve a case is a good idea. I want to get one for each mystery we solve. This is number three right, so what do you think I should get."

"Nothing." Spencer turned away and rested his head in his folded arms. "This better be it. I'm done putting my life on the line."

"Okay." It was her turn to roll her eyes.

"Done," he snapped.

END

Author's End Note

How was this one?

Years ago a friend of mine from culinary school went to the Philippines to work in a kitchen. 3 months later she was found like Tessa was. Authorities said it was suicide, but anyone who knew her thought different. As of the publication of this novel her family and friends have still not been satisfied with any answers.

I hope you liked this book. The next Alcrest Mystery will take you back to The Alcrest.

Please get in touch and tell me your thoughts.

Ways to find me

lorneoliverauthor@gmail.com
Facebook.com/oliverauthor
Facebook.com/TheAlcrestMysteries
And @LorneOliver on Twitter

You can get some Lorne Oliver news and merchandise
Lorneoliverauthor.weebly.com

The Alcrest BBQ Sauce

3 C	ketchup
1 C	brown sugar
1/3 C	apple cider vinegar
1 cup	butter, cubed
2 tbsp	smoked paprika
2 tbsp	garlic powder
1 tbsp	onion powder
1 tbsp	shallots
2 tsp	Cajun spice
2 tsp	cayenne
1 tbsp	Worcestershire sauce

1. Put everything into a sauce pan and whisk together. Heat until butter is melted. Let simmer for 20 minutes.

2. Can be stored in an airtight container in the refrigerator. Better the next day.